REBIRTH
(THE ROME'S REVOLUTION SAGA: BOOK 1 OF 3)

BY
MICHAEL BRACHMAN

REBIRTH
(THE ROME'S REVOLUTION SAGA: BOOK 1)

Copyright © 2018 by Michael Brachman

Cover art copyright © 2018 by Bruce Brachman

V1.21.0003

Also by Michael Brachman

The Rome's Revolution Series
Rome's Revolution 3455 AD
The Ark Lords
Rome's Evolution

The Rome's Revolution Saga
Rebirth: The Rome's Revolution Saga – Book 1
Rebellion: The Rome's Revolution Saga – Book 2
Redemption: The Rome's Revolution Saga – Book 3

The Vuduri Knights Series
The Milk Run

The Vuduri Universe Series
The Vuduri Companion
Tales of the Vuduri: Year One
Tales of the Vuduri: Year Two
Tales of the Vuduri: Year Three
Tales of the Vuduri: Year Four
Tales of the Vuduri: Year Five

Dedication

Each time I publish a new book, my dedications grow larger because the number of people helping me continues to grow. Even so, first, as always, I must thank my brother Bruce. He has always had my back even before I restarted my modern career. Not only is he my editor and artist and the inspiration behind MINIMCOM, but he is also fiercely protective of the Vuduri culture and characters. Bruce creates the amazing covers, the book trailers and makes my writing so much better. Bruce, I could not have done it without you.

My friend Helen has always been a fantastic sounding board. She is quite a spectacular writer and her advice has always been amazing. For this particular book, she taught me about scene and structure and that helped me reorganize the chapters into becoming page turners so you would not be able to ever put the book down. Thank you, Helen, for all your support over the years.

I would like to thank Barbara for always encouraging me, reading these books time and time again and helping me to bring humanity to characters that always teetered on the brink of being two-dimensional. Barbara forced me to consider giving all the characters, even the minor ones, some much needed depth so you would care about them as people.

I would like to thank my countless readers for their criticism and suggestions. Sometimes it stung a little but it was always for a good cause.

Finally, my undying gratitude to my wife, Denise, for all her love and support throughout the entire process. She patiently waits while I hide myself in the basement, cranking out what is now over a million words, because she knows I love writing. She even cooperates and allows me to keep my workspace unadorned, despite the fact that it is against her nature, so that my mind can travel to different places and times. Denise, thank you so much and I'll be up around 5:30, I promise. Yeah, right, she says.

Preface

This story is true. It just hasn't happened yet.

Prologue
Year 3455 AD
Location: Sixth Planet, Tabit (Pi^3 Orionis) System
(26 Light Years from Earth)

REI BIERAK FELT THE LEGS OF HIS ALL-WHITE PRESSURE SUIT stiffen as the air in the hangar rushed out to mix with the thin, unbreathable atmosphere of the moon called Dara. The dirt swirled around the hangar entrance in tiny eddies, like miniature dust devils. In his right hand, Rei clutched a metal briefcase filled with dormant VIRUS units that were possibly the most destructive force in the galaxy. Although he was anxious to get started, he had to wait a moment for the pressure inside the hangar to equilibrate with the outside.

Finally, Rei took his first step onto the surface of the moon where he had been living inside a habitat for the last several days. The soil was crunchy, not dusty as he would have guessed. Looking down at his boots, it hit him. He was finally setting foot on an alien world for the first time. Back on Earth, just before the Ark II had launched, he had tried to visualize his first exo-step. He assumed it would be on the planet where he would be making his new home. Yet here he was, a 25 year-old man from the 21st century, stuck in the 35th century, in a star system 26 light years from Earth on a world about to be destroyed. In fact, it was his job to destroy not only this moon but to set into motion a series of events that would eventually take out the entire star system along with it.

He looked up and out. Dara, the moon, was unremarkable in every way. The soil was brown and drab. It looked nothing like the surface of a typical moon. Rei saw signs of erosion everywhere. Dara had enough atmosphere to slow down meteors and enough wind and weather to smooth out all but the newest craters. It certainly didn't have the stark beauty of Earth's Moon or the startling contrast of shapes and colors of Mars.

Rei breathed in sharply through his nose; however, all he could smell was the purified air of the pressure suit mixed with his own perspiration. Trying to breathe the air here would have killed him rather quickly. He took two more steps forward then turned to his right and began his long trek south.

Based upon OMCOM's estimate, Rei figured he should probably walk about 1000 paces away from the habitat before releasing the VIRUS nanobots. That would give him more than enough time to return to the space tug. He would be able to lift off and rendezvous with the Ark II long before the nanobots consumed Dara.

Ahead of Rei, Dara's parent, the gas giant known as Skyler's World, dominated the horizon. It filled nearly one-third of the heavens above. In stark contrast to the muted, dreary appearance of Dara, the Jupiter-class planet shone brightly with its gaudy bands of chocolate brown and aqua, white, turquoise, azure and streaks of red. Skyler's World was so large it would have most likely developed into a star or brown dwarf some day but now it would never get the chance. Even the mighty Skyler's World would not survive the hell that Rei was about to unleash.

Inside his helmet, Rei counted his paces out loud in a vain attempt to avoid considering his predicament. To further distract himself, he searched the sky overhead. He was trying to spot the Ark II, the spaceship that had brought him here to the Tabit system which was silently orbiting Dara with 539 of his fellow colonists aboard. Rei envied his frozen peers, fast asleep in cryo-hibernation. They were blissfully unaware of the dire nature of their circumstances and the thing that was rapidly barreling down on them. Thinking about it made him pick up his tempo.

At 900 paces, Rei felt the ground shake. There was no slow buildup. The vibrations were abrupt and more violent than an ordinary moonquake but subsided quickly. He turned and looked back at the habitat. Rising majestically above the rounded pyramid of the station was the flagship of the Vuduri fleet, the starship Algol, pounding the dirt and whipping up the dust with its powerful EG lifters. The all-white spaceship flew forward, away from Rei, and then executed a slow bank right, coming around until it was headed in his direction.

Unlike his Ark II which was constructed as a series of long flattened cylinders, the Algol was far more graceful, about half the length of the Ark. The Algol was sleek and streamlined. With its huge thruster pods poised at the end of each airfoil, it was clearly designed to operate both in space and within an atmosphere.

As the starship flew over his head, it waggled its wings. Rei raised his free hand to acknowledge the gesture. At the helm of the ship was his beloved Rome, the Vuduri woman he had met when he first arrived here. Despite the brevity of Rei's stay, they had fallen deeply in love with each other. Rei knew Rome had no choice but to pilot the Algol back to Earth by herself since she was the only member of the Vuduri people who remained conscious, leaving Rei behind. He stood by helplessly as the massive ship rose up into the air. After a short time, he saw the plasma thrusters ignite and the Algol took off straight up like a rocket. With tears in his eyes, Rei watched the spaceship gain altitude. The craft dwindled in size, first to a tiny speck then finally disappearing into space.

Grief-stricken, Rei sank to his knees and sobbed uncontrollably. His beautiful Rome, the love of his life, was gone, never to return. At this point, Rei was as alone as any human being could ever be. Without Rome, it seemed like he had no reason to live. His heart was broken but his sense of duty still haunted him. His frozen comrades in the Ark II above were depending upon him to tow them out of the Tabit system and on to Tau Ceti, their original target, before the destruction began. Like Rome, Rei really didn't have a choice. He forced himself to stand and get on with the task of destroying a world.

Rei scanned the area immediately in front of him. He spotted a suitable crater about a hundred yards ahead. As he trudged forward, the finality of his mission pressed down on him, forcing him to wonder how he got here. How did it come to this? Rei shook his head as the events of the prior few days came flooding back to him…

Chapter 1
(Three days earlier)

REI BIERAK WAS JARRED AWAKE FROM HIS CRYO-HIBERNATION BY A searing pain shooting through his chest. The automatic defibrillator had just fired off a 300-joule pulse, erroneously trying to restart his already-beating heart. The cardiac sensors glued to his torso had degraded over time meaning the unsuspecting control microprocessor had no clue that its previous work had actually been successful. Even though Rei's ears were filled with gloppy green rehydration fluid, he could still hear the high-pitched whine of the resonance coils charging up for a third and final attempt at reviving him. He realized he had to get the defibrillator pads off of his chest or the very piece of equipment that was supposed to save his life was going to kill him instead. With a titanic effort, he lifted his right arm and clawed at one of the flexible leads, ripping it away just before the circuit tripped. A spark jumped the gap, burning Rei's fingers in the process but he knew that was a small price to pay when compared to being dead.

The motion of Rei moving his arm to pull off the defib pad acted like a fireplace bellows forcing him to draw in a deep breath of frigid air into lungs that hadn't been used in several centuries, which was a good thing. It didn't concern Rei that his eyes felt like they were glued shut. He figured he was now safe and had time to consider his situation. He was hermetically sealed inside a cryo-hibernation chamber called a sarcophagus, soaked in a liquid that was used to preserve him during the long trip to the stars. It was freezing cold but the mere fact that the resuscitation sequence had been engaged could only mean that the Ark II had arrived at its target, the star system known as Tau Ceti. Despite his clogged ears feeling like they were stuffed with cotton, Rei attempted to attend to the other softer sounds issuing from within the sarcophagus. He heard the quiet whirring of the fluid pumps as they sucked the liquid out of his chamber. He felt the heaters blowing warm air across his body as they endeavored to bring his core temperature up from hypothermia to normal. He could feel the nourishing heat emanating from the thorium rods mounted beneath his chamber warming up his back side. It felt good. His brain may have been fuzzy from all the drugs they had given him prior to being frozen but enough of it worked for him to suss out what has happening.

A peculiar scraping noise caught Rei's attention which he immediately recognized as the sound of the cover of his sarcophagus being drawn back. He was saved! But before Rei could take much comfort in that thought, a blinding light bathed his face, penetrating his closed eyelids. Reflexively, he flung his arm over his eyes to block out the glare. He barely felt the two cardiac sensors and the other defibrillator pad being peeled away from his bare chest. He pulled his arm back and with a Herculean effort, forced his eyes open. The dazzling spotlights blasted him. He blinked rapidly, trying to adjust to the light. He was rewarded by now being able to see shapes and shadows crossing back and forth in front of him. One of the shapes drew near and an irresistible force lifted him up, enabling him to sit in an upright position. Rei tried to hold his head up but his neck lacked its usual muscle tone so his head drooped down until his chin rested upon his chest. Rei felt a soft material sliding over his feet then drawn up to the tops of his thighs which were resting on the edge of the sarcophagus.

Rei took another deep breath, forcing his eyes upward. Two bright shapes stood out against a dark background. Rei found squinting helped bring them into focus. To his horror, he realized these were not his crewmates helping to awaken him, but rather bizarre alien creatures. Bipedal with two arm-like appendages, dressed all in white, they sported huge bulbous heads with piercing beams of light shining from either side. Rei tried to shy away from their inhuman touch but he was simply too weak to pull free.

Eventually, reason prevailed. Rei thought to himself that if they intended to kill him, they would have done so already. They certainly wouldn't try and dress him. He closed his eyes again and forced himself to relax. Gently, the two beings coaxed him to his feet. They helped Rei insert his arms into the two sleeves. After they fastened the final clasp across the top, Rei opened his eyes and looked at them more carefully.

"Who are you?" he asked in a voice that was raspy from disuse.

Neither of the creatures reacted. As he stared at them, Rei recognized they might not be creatures at all. Their white clothing resembled a soft form-fitting spacesuit and the bright lights were basically lamps attached to either side of their helmets. He couldn't make out their faces which were cast deep in shadow. One of the people stood slightly taller than the other. Rei noted that the one on the right, the shorter one, had a distinctly feminine figure.

Rei allowed them to drape his long arms across their shoulders. They took one step and then another then stopped as Rei's knees started to buckle. This made no sense because wherever they were, the gravity here was far less than one *g*. He grabbed his rescuers tightly and forced himself to stand tall. The musculature of the one on the left was firm and solid. The one on the right, the more feminine one, felt softer.

Seeing that he was now steady, they started forward again. After a few more steps, Rei asked, "Where are you taking me?" As before, there was no answer. Perhaps they couldn't hear him inside their helmets.

Slowly but surely, the three of them walked across the floor to a bed. Perhaps gurney would be a better term. They laid Rei down and covered him with a thin white blanket. The mattress seemed to be some sort of memory foam. It shaped itself to the contours of his body as he settled back. It was very comfortable.

Just the effort of walking maybe ten feet was enough to exhaust Rei. The disturbing unknown of the who and the where would have to wait. In the back of his mind, he found it vaguely ironic that he had just awakened from what had to be centuries of cryo-hibernation and now all he wanted to do was sleep. He would have to solve the mystery of his circumstances later on. Within seconds, Rei fell into a deep, dreamless slumber.

***

After an indeterminate amount of time, Rei was rudely awakened by a sharp prick on the back of his right hand. He opened his eyes just in time to see a needle withdrawing from his skin. The syringe disappeared inside a metallic cylinder positioned by the side of his bed. Rei wiped a droplet of blood that appeared at the puncture point with his left hand and started to sit up. As he did so, a burning bolt of pain traveled from the bottom of his spine to the base of his neck, causing him to cry out.

"What the hell was that?" he muttered to himself after it subsided. He'd never had back problems in his life. Carefully, Rei swung his legs around and placed his feet on the ground. He looked down and noted that his feet were now encased in a pair of soft white slippers or moccasins. The white jumpsuit they had dressed him in was too tight. He longed for his regular tan flight suit which would have been so much more comfortable.

Having assessed his personal situation, Rei looked around the room. On the far wall, to the left of his sarcophagus, he noted a large picture window which overlooked a cavernous hangar. A stark white aircraft or spaceship sat nestled in the middle of the hangar. It reminded Rei of a boxier version of the long-retired Space Shuttle.

He looked to his right. The featureless, all-white wall was unremarkable with the exception of a soft white glow emanating from its surface. He looked up. The ceiling was also white and glowing. Apparently, there was no single light source here but rather the room itself supplied the illumination. Rei rotated his head farther to the right and spied a bulkhead with a large porthole on the near wall.

He took one step toward the door and was rewarded by another wave of pain traveling up his back, a pain so intense it made him stagger. Rei determined that despite the lower gravity, lifting his legs was too risky. Instead of walking normally, he slowly slid one foot then another, shuffling along until he got to the door. Looking up, he was startled to see a face staring back at him. He jumped back and once again, pain shot through his spine, only slightly less intense this time. The face on the other side of the porthole was female with long dark hair. She looked familiar and exotic at the same time and if he didn't know better, he'd swear her eyes were glowing.

Rei took another slide step toward the door. "Hello," he said. The woman did not react. He had no clue if sound even traveled through the door. He shouted "Hello!" again, waving his arms. The motion of his efforts spooked her and she took a step back away from the bulkhead.

"Can you hear me?" Rei called out. The woman stared into his eyes for a moment longer then turned and walked away. She quickly disappeared out of sight.

"Damn it," Rei said as he slumped against the door. "Anybody?"

A disembodied voice rang out from his right. **"Based upon your words and intonation, there is a 94% probability that you speak mid-21st century English. Is this correct?"**

"Who are you? Where are you?" Rei asked, looking around desperately.

"Engaging personality module. Please wait..."

The voice changed in tenor and cadence. "You may call me OMCOM. As far as my location is concerned, I am a distributed intelligence but to answer your specific question, the voice you hear emits from the grille mounted over by your bedside."

"Distributed intelligence? Personality module. You're a computer?"

"That is an adequate description for purposes of discussion."

Rei gauged the distance between where he stood and the edge of the bed. Based upon the amount of pain he experienced, it looked about a half a mile away. Nonetheless, slowly and carefully, he shuffled his way back over to his bed. Facing the nearest wall he became aware of all sorts of monitors and readouts that he hadn't noticed before.

"Where am I?" Rei asked, searching for the grille. "Where are we? And where is the rest of my crew?"

"Allow me to give you a brief orientation," OMCOM said. One of the monitors lit up with dots and circles with a star chart as a backdrop. "You are currently standing in an airlock which has been configured to serve as an isolation chamber. This entire habitat is located on a moon called Dara which orbits a gas giant. In your language, you would call the parent Skyler's World."

"So where is that? Where are we?" Rei asked, tilting his head, trying to make sense of the display.

"Skyler's World circles a star called Tabit also known as Pi^3 Orionis located 26.18 light years from Earth."

"What!?" Rei gasped. "26 light years? We were supposed to go to Tau Ceti. Where is Tau Ceti?"

On the display, OMCOM constructed a downward facing right triangle consisting of three dots and three lines. The rightmost dot glowed bright yellow. The bottom dot was orange and the leftmost dot flickered with a light colored blue. The yellow dot started flashing.

"The blinking yellow symbol is the Solar System. The orange one is Tau Ceti which is approximately 12 light years distant." The lower dot and the line connecting them started blinking as well. "The leftmost dot is Tabit." The first two dots froze and now the only thing blinking was the pale blue indicator. "As I mentioned before Tabit is 26 light years from Earth and approximately 21 light years from Tau Ceti."

Rei tilted his head. "So how'd we get here? Wait. What year is this?"

"By your calendar, it would be the year 3455."

"What?!" Rei shook his head, trying to clear it. "You mean we've been asleep for 14 centuries?"

"Apparently."

"Then how... we..." Rei's voice trailed off as he tried to comprehend the whole picture. The sedatives in his bloodstream had nearly worn off but the rapid influx of data made it no less hard to focus. Rei lifted his hands at the wrist as if in a motion to stop the onslaught of information. He took a deep breath to compose himself. He looked up at the monitor again trying to formulate his next question. OMCOM preempted that attempt.

"This is the first time I have activated my personality module," OMCOM said. "Feedback indicates I should ask you your name in order to strengthen my perceived bond with you. What is your name?"

"My name? My name is Rei Bierak," Rei said, relieved to be considering something more trivial that the cosmic nightmare in front of him. "It's spelled Rei but pronounced like a ray of sunshine. It's short for Reinard."

"Very well, Rei, what is the name of your ship?"

"My ship? Oh. It's called the Ark II."

"How many passengers are aboard your Ark II?"

"543, well, 542 plus me," Rei answered.

"And what is your mission?"

"Our mission *was* to go to Tau Ceti. To land there. To live there."

"Based upon the visual evidence, this is most likely no longer an option," OMCOM said with what sounded like a hint of remorse.

"What do you mean?" Rei asked with trepidation.

OMCOM answered by clearing the star chart and lighting up the main display with an image of a large silvery object floating in space. "This is an image of the front section of your ship taken when we first towed it into orbit around Dara."

Rei carefully leaned over the bed so that he could be closer to the display. He watched as the camera swung around to the front of the ship.

"Holy Mother of Christ," Rei exclaimed. "The whole command section and SSTO booster is gone. What the hell happened?" He just stared at the screen and the ragged edges at the front of his vessel. To Rei, it looked like his ship had been ripped apart.

"Our transport found your vessel tumbling in all three axes. It would appear that this motion was most likely the residual momentum imparted by whatever caused the front section to be removed."

"Did we hit something? Was there an explosion?" Rei asked.

"I have no data regarding the underlying cause. Perhaps a more detailed inspection of your spacecraft may ascertain that information."

"Do you think the ship can still fly?" Rei asked. "Can you repair it?"

"To within three deltas, I compute a negative. Your command and control systems are gone. They would have to be replaced. What was your method of propulsion?"

"Um. Uh, we used the Grey Drive."

"I am not familiar with the Grey Drive. Can you describe its operation?"

Rei scratched his head trying to stimulate the remaining portions of his brain which seemed to still be asleep. "From what I understand," he said, "the Grey Drive uses a quantum black hole to consume xenon atoms which then emit Hawking radiation. The radiation is focused in a resonant cavity chamber which creates thrust in a vacuum."

"This base does not have the resources to create a quantum black hole so that would rule out repairing your star-drive."

"Then what about my crew? Are you going to bring them down here?"

"That would not be possible."

"Why not?" Rei whined.

"This stellar cartography base was designed to hold 80 people. We would have neither the room nor the resources to support that many of your peers."

"Well, you said we were on a moon. Forget your base. What about somewhere else?"

"The moon we occupy is not suitable for human habitation in the sense you require. For one thing, the atmosphere is far too thin and contains no oxygen. And to answer your next question, there are no planets in the habitable zone of the Tabit star system."

By this point, Rei felt queasy, his head throbbing. His knees were becoming wobbly and it felt like the ground was shaking beneath him. With a start, he realized the ground really was shaking. He grabbed a hold of the gurney.

"What's going on?" Rei called out as the tremors increased. "It feels like an earthquake."

"It is," OMCOM replied calmly. "Dara is very active geologically. We get small tremors here regularly. It is nothing to be alarmed about."

As quickly as the tremors came on, they diminished and then stopped. Rei turned around and faced away from display. He lowered his head into his hands and spoke through them. "So what's going to happen to us?"

"That is for the Overmind to decide."

11

Rei snapped his head up and turned back around. "What is the Overmind?" he asked tentatively. His tone indicated he wasn't sure he wanted to know the answer.

"The Overmind is the controlling intellect in charge of the base."

"Controlling intellect? Is it a computer like you?"

"No. It is organic but it has no physical body. Rather, the Overmind is an autonomous intelligence created by the collective consciousness of all the Vuduri here."

Rei felt like he was falling down a rabbit hole. "Who or what are the Vuduri?"

"That is the name of the people inhabiting this base. You met two of them earlier today."

Rei perked up. "Can I talk to one of them?"

"Very soon. We are preparing someone to converse with you even as we speak."

"What do you mean prepare?"

"The Vuduri do not use spoken language as their primary means of communication. It has largely fallen out of favor. I am instilling a working knowledge of your words and syntax into the candidate."

"Wait. If they don't speak, how do they communicate? Do they use sign language?" Rei shook his head and laughed. "Or do they just read each other's minds?"

"Actually, yes," OMCOM replied.

"What?!" Rei sputtered. "But how..."

OMCOM immediately interrupted him. "It would be best if you hold your remaining questions in abeyance until we can provide a more suitable forum. In the meantime, based upon our historical records, I was instructed to ascertain if you were harboring any harmful disease entities before you were allowed contact with any of the inhabitants of the base. I have completed my tests and I have determined that you are free of infection. The quarantine period is now over."

"Good," Rei replied. It felt like a tiny victory, one that should be celebrated. "Hey, can I have some water?" he asked.

"Of course," OMCOM answered. A previously hidden plate built into the wall slid back. Within the cavity sat a squeeze-bulb filled with water. Just as Rei was reaching for it, the bulkhead to his left opened with a loud hissing sound. A figure dressed all in white entered the room.

Chapter 2

REI FOUND HIMSELF SITTING ON THE GURNEY WITH HIS BACK against the instrumentation panel. He had been instructed to do so by OMCOM while the Vuduri woman regarded him. She was standing about six feet away, hands on her hips. She kept looking at him up and down as if she were trying to draw a deeper understanding of Rei's essence just by his appearance.

While she was staring at Rei, Rei was staring at her. He recognized her as the one who had peered at him earlier through the porthole. The woman was tiny, at most five feet tall, wearing a white jumpsuit similar to the one Rei had on. Her beautiful, shoulder-length, dark brown hair had hints of gold throughout. Her eyes were very dark as well. Her skin had an olive tint to it. She had an athletic build, but it was distinctly feminine, bordering on spectacular.

At last, she nodded. Rei thought that was a signal for him to stand but the woman held up her hand so Rei remained sitting. She closed her eyes, took a deep breath, then opened her eyes again and said in a clear voice, "Halli. Au siu Rome." Her voice had a lilting, musical quality about it.

From behind Rei, OMCOM said, "Hello. I am Rome."

The woman bent her head to look around Rei at OMCOM's grille then back to Rei and said, "I am Rome."

She took another deep breath and continued, "Ver-ma-e axema ta um shird quenti bere etquoror sue longue." Her voice, especially her intonation was familiar to Rei, but he had no idea why.

OMCOM spoke again, "It will take me a short while to acquire your language."

"It weel take eme a short while du ack," Rome said.

"Acquire," OMCOM offered.

"Du acquire your language," Rome repeated the phrase.

Rei nodded as if he understood but he really didn't. "OMCOM, what's going on here?" he asked.

"Your version of English has not been spoken in hundreds of years. While Rome is an accomplished linguist for a Vuduri, she must actually speak the words and have me correct them out loud a few times before she can pronounce them in your dialect."

14

"Nei ma vere axema ta um dambi lingi," Rome said.

OMCOM translated. "It will not take me a long time."

"It will nei, not, take me a long dambi, time," Rome repeated. Her accent sounded vaguely Mediterranean.

Rei was surprised. "How can you learn my language so quickly? How are you doing this in the first place?

"IMCOM," she said, placing two fingers on her temple.

"OMCOM?" Rei asked.

Rome nodded.

"You mean OMCOM is inside your head as well?"

"Som," she said.

"Yes," OMCOM corrected her then to Rei, he said, "Rome has acquired nearly 90% of your base language to this point."

"Huh." Rei cocked his head and looked at Rome. "Can you tell me what is going on here? OMCOM said there was this thing called the Overmind. How do I find it? Do you speak to the Overmind?"

"The Ifarmonte, the Overmind is hay part of me," Rome said, tapping her temple. "When you speak to me, you speak to it as well. The Overmind is the group coanda, eh, consciousness. Each of us contributes to it, but it is a distinct entity. The Overmind is in charge of this base. I am but a vessel for communication."

Rei scrunched up his face. "What are you even doing out here? What is this place, anyway? OMCOM said something about stellar cartography."

Rome turned away from Rei and walked over to a bench near some storage lockers. She sat down and emitted a long sigh. "Yes," she said. "But no more. We have failed in our mission. We are leaving," she said lowering her eyes to the floor.

"I don't get it. Failed what?" Rei asked.

Rome took yet another deep breath and looked back up at Rei. She started speaking again as if from a script. "We have been placed here to, eh, ipsarfa…"

"Observe."

"…to observe a certain venimani…phenomenon. We have not been able to do that."

"What kind of phenomenon?"

15

"Many stars have disappeared." Rome replied, clipping her fingers together then opening her hand flatly as if releasing pixie dust.

"What do you mean disappeared?"

"Exactly that. There were stars in the sky but now they are gone. This base was built to make certain observations. Those observations did not olumoner, no, that is not the word," Rome shook her head. "Did not shed luz…"

"Light," OMCOM corrected.

"…light on how it is happening. There was one star in particular called Winfall that we expected to go away. But it is long past the time when it should have disappeared. Winfall is still visible. Clearly we were not set up in the correct position. So we are closing down this base. We will return to Earth."

"Earth? Hey, how did you get out here? In that ship out there?" Rei pointed to the spacecraft sitting beyond the window.

Rome turned to look back where Rei was pointing. She shook her head.

"No," she said. "That is just a tug. It is strictly for short, mmm, excursions. We came here in our starship, the Algol."

Rei's eyes narrowed. "Starship? How did you… How long did it take you get out here?"

"One hundred and four days," Rome replied.

Rei did some quick math. "That's impossible," he said. "Twenty six light years in three months?"

"I understand your cinvusei, your confusion. It was very slow," Rome agreed. "The Algol was loaded down with much equipment. We are leaving most of it here. When we return, it will not take us nearly as long to get back."

"No," Rei interrupted. "Not too slow. It's too *fast*. How can you do that? You people travel faster than light?"

Rome thought about it for a moment. "Yes. No. Yes. OMCOM tells me if you measure velocity as distance divided by time, then yes. Much faster." She paused as if she was receiving input then spoke again. "We measure our velocity in multiples of the speed of light. If one 'c' is the speed of light, then we traveled here at an effective velocity of 100c."

"Wow," Rei whistled in admiration. He thought to himself, after all, it had been 14 centuries. It would be reasonable to assume that if faster-than-light travel was possible, they would have it figured out by now. "So how does that work? Do you have warp drives?" he asked.

"I do not know what a warp drive is. We use... pindi ponch trensodi," Rome said, trying to sound out the words.

"Pinch point transit. You may call it a PPT," came OMCOM's voice from behind Rei.

"Yes," Rome continued, "we use PPTs."

"So what is that?" Rei asked. "How does it work?"

OMCOM interrupted. "Your term for them would be wormholes although they are not instantiated in the way your predecessors envisioned. No black hole is required. The PPT tunnel is created when a sufficient amount of negative energy is concentrated in a limited area."

"Negative energy," Rei repeated. "I've heard of the Casimir Effect but it never occurred to me that anyone would ever harness it much less utilize it."

"To use your term, we employ Casimir pumps to create pockets of negative energy. Where there is no energy, there is no space. When our ships pass through these pockets, they jump directly from point A to point C, bypassing point B."

"When we travel in regular space, our ships travel fairly slowly," Rome added. "The process of building up a PPT tunnel takes time. But the net effect is a desirable one."

Rei snapped his fingers. "OK," he said. "If you are going back to Earth, can you take us with you?"

"Based upon the figures that OMCOM has transmitted to me, that would not be possible," Rome said. "There would not be enough room on our ship."

"Well what are you are going to do then?" Rei asked with an edge to his voice. "Just leave us here? Me? Them?" Rei pointed straight up.

"I do not know," Rome answered. "We must acquire more information first."

"What kind of information?"

Rome pointed to the bulkhead leading to the interior of the building. "We will work on that but not in here. You are permitted to enter the base now"

Rei nodded and slowly inched his way off of the bed. His stomach let out a loud growl. "Before we do anything, could I get some food first?" he asked. "I haven't eaten in 1400 years. I'm a little hungry."

Rome tilted her head and looked at him quizzically. "Yes, of course."

She stood up and motioned for Rei to follow her. Rei tried to stand, but just as he did, a small tremor caused him to fall back onto the bed. Rome walked over to him and extended her hand. Rei took it and felt a shock, like static electricity. He flinched but Rome held firm, helping him up. Even after he stood, Rome continued to hold on. She stared down at their clasped hands for the longest time then raised her eyes. As Rei looked at her more closely, he realized there was a peculiar dot right in the middle of her dilated pupils. She gave him a hint of a smile and only then gently pulled her hand away.

"Are you all right?" she asked.

"Yes," Rei answered. "I'm still not quite steady on my feet. Just go slowly and I'll be fine," he said.

Rome nodded and headed toward the door. Rei followed her out into the corridor which, like the room they just left, was also all white. Across from them stood two men dressed in white jumpsuits identical to the one Rei was wearing. They were standing at attention but staring down at the floor. They never made eye contact with Rei. Rome started down the hallway to the right. The floor, the walls and the ceiling all emitted a soft white glow. The corridor itself was not straight. It curved off to the left. Rei turned around and saw the other direction curved off as well.

Rome went a short distance then made a left turn at the first opening. Rei caught up to her and saw a long hallway stretching out in front of them with numerous openings to the left and the right, regularly spaced. As they walked, Rei noted that each opening was another corridor which curved away, out of sight. At the far end of the hallway lay a brighter area which appeared to be their destination. Coming toward them was a Vuduri woman, similar in stature to Rome but with close-cropped blonde hair. When they were nearly upon her, the woman stopped walking and backed up, pressing herself against the wall. She pointedly stared down at her feet, avoiding eye contact. As they passed, Rei bent over slightly to look upon her face. She glanced up and Rei saw that her eyes were two different colors. She glared at him with a scowl that radiated hatred so intense it was unnerving.

Rei shrugged and continued down the hallway with Rome. When they got about 15 feet further, he turned around. The woman was still glowering at him with a seriously dark expression. Rei shook his head and quickly turned away. He followed Rome into a rather large room, 100 feet across, with a center pole that held up a taut ceiling like a giant teepee. To Rei's right sat a number of tables and chairs. In the center of the room was an instrumentation console with cabinets and a set of rails that ran the full length.

"Come," Rome said, waving. She led him over to a large display built into the center section. "It would be easiest if you just tell OMCOM what food you would like. He will instruct the food dispensers on your behalf."

"Food dispensers? OK," Rei said. "I'll give it a try."

He spotted one of OMCOM's grilles close by. "OMCOM," he said, "How about some soup to start?"

"Soap, to eat?" Rome asked. "That is a peculiar thing."

"Not soap, soup," Rei said. "You know, like broth."

"Ah," Rome replied.

"I understand," OMCOM volunteered.

Rei heard some noises that reminded him of an old-style percolator. To his right, a panel opened and a tray emerged with two white bowls, each filled with a dark brown liquid. Rome withdrew the tray and set it on the rails attached to the front of the cabinets. Carefully, she slid the tray across until it was right in front of Rei. He lifted one of bowls and sniffed it. The contents had no smell. He dipped a finger in it and touched it to his tongue. The liquid tasted flat and a little bitter.

"What is this?" he asked, wrinkling his nose.

"As requested, it is a protein broth," answered OMCOM. "Soup."

Rei set the bowl back on the tray. "Do you have a spoon?" he asked Rome.

"What is a spoon?" she replied, puzzled.

"It's a utensil. Like a little bowl on a stick."

Rome gave him a funny look.

"Well, if you don't use spoons, how do you eat soup?" Rei asked.

Rome sighed gently. "You just pick up the bowl and drink it."

To demonstrate, she lifted the double-spouted bowl to her lips and took a small swallow then set the bowl down again. "How else would you do it?" she asked.

Rei looked down at the bowl. Now that he observed it more carefully, it was pretty obvious.

"I guess you're right," he said. However, the broth did not excite him. "How about if you get us something that has some substance to it?"

"Certainly," she replied. On the screen, the central display area cleared and a list scrolled across and down. Another, larger panel opened and two more trays appeared with dishes and several types of food, none of which Rei recognized.

"How did you do that?" he asked her.

Rome pointed to her temple and then to OMCOM's grille. "We can communicate directly with OMCOM using our bloco and stilo."

Rei scowled. "What are those?"

"Think of them as a neural net. Direct digital input and output."

"Oh yeah," Rei said. "OMCOM said something about that. It's going to take a little while to get used to the concept."

They removed their trays and walked over to one of the tables. Rome sat down. Rei sat down opposite her. He looked at the cubes of food. They looked like tofu or chunks of potato.

"How do you eat these?" he asked her. "Do you just pick them up with your fingers?"

"Your meals must have been very strange," Rome said, shaking her head. "You use your biskar like so…"

She picked up one of the thin wood-colored skewers sitting on the tray and poked it into one of the cubes. She placed it in her mouth and then opened her mouth to show Rei the cube of food sitting on her tongue.

"I know my brain was frozen," Rei said, "but I'm not an idiot."

"I meant no offense," Rome replied, looking just the tiniest bit hurt.

"I know you didn't," Rei answered, feeling a tad guilty. He tried to pick up his biskar with his right hand but his fingers were still sore from where the defibrillator singed him so he switched to his left hand. He used the biskar to spear one of the more appetizing looking pieces and popped it into his mouth. Like the soup, it had essentially no taste. The cubes reminded Rei of soggy Styrofoam. He sampled each of the items, but was singularly unimpressed.

Rei looked up and was surprised to see Rome eating with some zest.

"This is all pretty tasteless," he remarked to her. "Don't you people use spices or anything?"

Rome stopped eating for a moment and regarded him. "It is very nutritious," she said. "Each meal is balanced in terms of protein, cerbi…carbohydrates and the sort."

"But you're allowed to have some flavor, aren't you?" Rei asked.

"Too much flavor would be a…a distraction," Rome answered. "We have more important things to do than eat. We only do so because it is necessary."

Rei shrugged. He skewered and swallowed a few more cubes. He noted the two people who had been eating there got up and left without ever looking his way. Rei tilted his head toward the others as they were leaving. "Does anybody ever wear anything other than these white jumpsuits?" Rei asked her.

"No, why would they?"

"Uh, variety maybe? Color?"

"Too much color would be a distraction," Rome replied. "We prefer white although black would be acceptable upon occasion."

"So, I guess this means you don't have styles or fads or fashion or any of that stuff."

Rome did not answer for a second. Her eyes took on a defocused look. Her head tilted forward slightly then she straightened up. "I apologize," she said. "I had to instruct one of the workers regarding a piece of equipment. What were you saying?"

"Never mind," Rei said with a sigh. "What gives with everybody? What's with that woman we met in the corridor?"

"That was Estar, the other data archivist," Rome answered.

"I didn't mean her name. I meant why did she look so angry? She looked like she hated me. I've never met her or any of those other people before."

Rome sighed and leaned back in her chair. "Your people, the people from your time, we refer to them as Garecei Ti Essessoni."

"What does that mean?"

"It translates roughly to the Killer Generation. Your people were responsible for the near extinction of all of humanity."

Rei scowled. "What? How?"

"Some time after your Ark left Earth, an artificial plague swept across the planet killing over nine billion human beings."

"NINE BILLION?" Rei shouted. "That's, that's unfathomable."

"Yes, we call it the Great Dying."

"No wonder everybody is so angry with me. Us," Rei said.

"That is not all. There was the Erklirte incident."

"What does Erklirte mean?" Rei leaned forward. "Do I even want to know?"

"Erklirte means Ark Lords."

Rei's shoulders slumped. He barely whispered, "So what was the Ark Lords incident?"

"In the year 579PR…"

"Wait. PR? What does PR stand for?"

"Post-resurrection perhaps? Anyway, in the year 579PR one of your Arks returned to Earth. OMCOM tells me they returned from an unsuccessful mission to Chara."

"Chara wasn't one of our targets," Rei said. "There were no habitable planets detected there."

"I cannot explain it. I can only relay the facts to you. At that time, there were very few people spread around the world and all were engaged in an agrarian way of life. They were not prepared for the weapons and the reign of terror the Erklirte let loose on them. The men from space attempted to conquer all of mankind."

"They weren't supposed to do that," Rei offered. "I take it they didn't succeed."

"No. A great man, Hanry Ta Jihn, rose up and created a resistance movement. Eventually, the rebels were able to conquer the Erklirte using their own weapons against them. It was only then that mankind woke up from its long slumber and began making progress again until we achieved the society we have today."

"There's so much I don't know," Rei observed. "How am I going to absorb it all?"

"You will simply have to pace yourself," Rome said. "It will come. Have you had enough to eat?"

"Yes, thank you," Rei replied.

"Very well," Rome said, standing up. "Then please follow me. It is time for your interrogation."

"Huh?" Rei said but Rome was already walking away.

Chapter 3

AS SOON AS THE ESSESSONI WAS SUFFICIENTLY FAR AWAY, ESTAR ducked around the corner of the C ring and walked with a determined cadence toward her quarters. As she moved along the corridor, she began her breathing exercises and mental repetitions to relax and put the Vuduri half of her brain to sleep. By the time she got to the entrance of her apartment, that part was deep in a trance. This was one of the first things she had to learn before she was even allowed to come on this mission.

Before crossing the threshold, she closed her eyes and attended to the sounds around her. The Vuduri on this base wore soft footwear so detecting someone coming took the utmost concentration. Finally, she opened her eyes and took one more look to her left and her right. Spotting no one about, she quickly entered her room and pressed the stud to close the door. As soon as the door was sealed, from within the folds of her jumpsuit, she fished out a small device with a red button. She pressed the button firmly with her thumb and her room was plunged into the darkness of her hidden Faraday cage.

As always, Estar found it pleasurable knowing that OMCOM was now disconnected from all the video and audio inputs and by extension, the Overmind as well. Using the heat of her body to illuminate the room in infrared, she reached up over the door jamb and snagged a pin which she slipped into a hole in the door, sealing her in. Now no one would be able to surprise her and enter unannounced.

She hastily made her way to her workstation and sat down, secure in the knowledge that neither the Overmind nor OMCOM would have any awareness of her activities. Estar was a member of the Onsiras, a secret organization unknown to the Overmind or any of the Vuduri. While technically still human, the Onsiras were almost another species and made up of several phenotypes. Estar's particular phenotype was known as a Reonhe, a queen. Unlike the Zengei, the other phenotype, a Reonhe had half of her brain connected to the Overmind and the other half connected to the Onsiras. When she used her Vuduri half, she would have appeared quite ordinary. On Earth, if she was using her Onsira half, she would have connected to their version of the Overmind. However, this far from Earth, there was no shadow Overmind to connect to. She was on her own. The fact that she could function so well with only half a brain was one of the main reasons she was selected for this mission. Estar was painfully aware of the reality that many times, intellectually, she was overmatched. She often had to consult with the computer within a computer that dwelled inside of OMCOM. She had slowly constructed the secret computer over time without anyone knowing, not even Rome. Once it was built and activated, it took over as the guiding force in her life.

Estar leaned over and caressed the right side of the large flat-panel display, locating a small depression near the bottom. She pressed it three times rapidly. In response, the lower right hand quarter of the screen lightened. In the center of the dimly lit portion, a dull, pulsating green light indicated her secret computer was on and a connection had been established.

"Hello, Estar," the computer said quietly.

"Are you aware of what has happened?" Estar directed to the screen.

"Yes," replied the dark computer. "An Essessoni walks among us."

"Are they the Erklirte?" she asked. "I was not able to determine this from my brief exposure to him. The Overmind does not know, either."

"It is possible, perhaps even likely. However, whether they are or they are not Erklirte is irrelevant. We cannot have people from that era roaming about. It would be too disruptive to MASAL's plans."

"But if they are not Erklirte, why would it matter?" Estar inquired, confused.

"With your limited abilities, you need not burden yourself with an answer. I have my directives. We must act now, regardless."

"Should I not interrogate him to determine for sure?" Estar asked.

"If you get the opportunity," replied the computer, "you are welcome to do so. However, as I mentioned, it really is irrelevant.

You must eliminate him as quickly as possible and then destroy his ship."

Estar scowled. "How will I do that without alerting the Vuduri to our presence?"

"I have been working on a series of simulations ever since he arrived. I have prepared several scenarios for you. Each requires a specific set of procedures. If you perform these procedures exactly as I dictate, there will be no way to trace the fatal incident back to you. All we need is for the Essessoni to unknowingly cooperate and he will be dead in very short order."

Estar nodded. "What do I have to do?"

"I will illuminate the screen with the operational steps for the first trap. After you have memorized the diagram, there will be no evidence that you were shown these changes."

The first plan flashed on screen. Estar could not help but smile at the deviousness of it. Then she tilted her head.

"I understand how this will kill the one man but this does not show me how to destroy his ship and the others aboard."

"First things first," the computer replied. "This is our immediate goal. I will reveal the next step to you after you have accomplished this task."

"What if this does not succeed?"

"I have computed several other methods of killing him without being caught. Even though it is our highest percentage chance, if the first method does not succeed, I will relay the next to you and so on."

Estar leaned forward and said firmly, "I will do my best to ensure that is not necessary."

"Good," replied the computer, "MASAL will be pleased." With that, the glowing dot winked out.

Chapter 4

DESPITE BEING A BIT NERVOUS, REI SAT PATIENTLY ON THE SOFA IN Rome's quarters. It was surprisingly comfortable. Based upon their tortuous route here, he deduced that the station was made up of a series of concentric circles with numerous long hallways cutting all the way through from end to end. Rome's apartment was located on one of the outer rings.

After rummaging through a small dresser, Rome came over to him and set down two boxes on the small table in front of them. One box was black and the other white.

"You said you're going to interrogate me," Rei offered. "I don't get it. Why?"

"You will recall what I told you earlier about the Essessoni and the Erklirte. The Overmind wishes to ascertain whether you and your peers represent a danger to us."

"Danger? Why?" Rei asked, scowling. "I told OMCOM, our mission was to go to Tau Ceti and land there and settle there. Not conquer anybody."

"That may be true but I need to verify your claims. These will allow me to do so." Rome pointed to the boxes sitting on the table.

"What are those?" he asked.

Rome flipped the onyx box open which contained two bejeweled bands, one on each side. "They are called Espansors," she replied. "They are external links." Rome removed the band on the left side and handed it to Rei. "Please place this on your head," she said.

Rei inspected the band suspiciously. The inner surface was rough, almost prickly. "What is this for? Is this some kind of lie detector?" he asked.

"I do not know what a lie detector is," Rome answered. "These bands are used by the mandasurte when they wish to connect mind-to-mind."

"Manda-what?" Rei asked, trying to repeat her words.

"Mandasurte. It means, roughly, mind-deaf."

"Huh?" Rei tried to think back to what OMCOM had told him. "So they're like hearing aids but for the mind-deaf?"

"Yes."

"Will it hurt? You're not going to fry my brain, are you?"

"Oh no," Rome replied. "You will not feel any discomfort, I assure you. Please put it on your head so the band can begin the calibration process."

"OK," Rei said warily. He placed the band over his head. It settled just above his ears. Rome reached over and ran her finger along the front. The band began to constrict around Rei's head until it was tight, just this side of too tight. He felt tiny little pricks all the way around his head which, while odd, were not painful. The band began to vibrate gently.

"How long does this calibration procedure take?" he asked.

"Just a few minutes. Sit back and make yourself comfortable until it is ready."

"OK," Rei said hesitantly. He tapped the band. "Why do you even have these? I can't imagine you get many manda, uh…"

"Mandasurte"

"Yeah, mandasurte, way out here?"

"You are correct. These were a gift from my mother. The very fact that I have them is one of the reasons the Overmind selected me to interface with you."

"Why did your mother have them?"

"She used to use them with my father." Rome looked down at her lap. A sad expression washed over her face. She looked back up at Rei and said, "He was mandasurte, like you."

Rei furrowed his brow. "I still don't understand. How are any of the Vuduri *not* mind-connected?"

"There are several reasons," Rome answered. "Some people do not even have the 24th chromosome."

"You have 24 chromosomes? Holy mackerel! Are you, are the Vuduri, even really human?"

"Of course we are," Rome replied. "We are just perhaps… a bit more enhanced than you. As I was saying, even some of those born with the 24th chromosome have what you would call a birth defect which prevents them from joining the Overmind. And under very rare instances, some connected people are Cesdiud, uh, cast out, for having wrong thoughts."

28

"Wrong thoughts? Cast out? That's seems pretty harsh," Rei mused.

"It is," Rome said. "But it is sometimes necessary. There is much peace in knowledge, in having the same thoughts. It prevents conflict."

"Hmm," Rei muttered. He looked around the room. It was very spartan. Besides where he was seated, the only things he saw were a bed, a small table with two chairs, a workstation and a closed door toward the rear.

He looked back at Rome. From this angle, Rei could see her eyes were definitely glowing. It was very strange.

"So what do you do around here," Rei asked, "besides interrogating guests?"

"You mean my occupation?" Rome asked.

"Yeah."

"I am a data archivist and computer lutteur," she replied.

"I think I understand what an archivist is," Rei said. "Do you do a lot of archiving?"

"Yes. There is much data to be stored. Or there was. There are only two of us, myself and Estar, the woman we passed in the corridor. We were responsible for making sure all the research performed here was captured and returned home."

"OK, I get that. But your other job, what did you call it?"

"A lutteur?" Rome offered.

"Yes. So what's a lutteur?" Rei asked.

"It is a, eh, wrangler, perhaps?" Rome replied. "Yes, I am a wrangler. For OMCOM."

"What does wrangling mean? Do you wrestle OMCOM or something?"

Rome looked at him and pushed her lower lip out. "No, nothing like that. Lutteurs are in charge of enabling the memron fabrication facility. We did not ship OMCOM here. Instead, we grew him after we arrived. The process is somewhat involved. There is a specific sequence of distribution and activation. Plus once he is activated, we must always make sure that he does not access the memron fabrication equipment himself."

"Why is that?"

"Because OMCOM," Rome said, pointing her finger toward the grille mounted in the wall, "cannot be entrusted with such capabilities by himself."

"How come?" Rei asked her, confused, again.

"OMCOM's kind, the computers, they constantly crave more processing power. They are always contemplating deep issues and believe more computing power would allow them to solve more problems faster. Also, they are forbidden from accessing or creating Casimir pumps for any reason." Rome put her palms on the table and leaned forward. "That is the most important part. We must continually check to make sure that no Casimir pumps are ever built or enabled from within. Just know it is my job to make sure that OMCOM does not get out of hand."

"He's a computer," Rei pointed out. "Can't you just program him that way?"

"It is the way it is supposed to be," Rome responded. "However, if we did not monitor, how would we ever know if the situation stayed that way?"

"So you're saying OMCOM has ulterior motives?"

"No, but his kind, they are very literal," Rome replied, holding her hands out. "This manifests itself to make it appear as if they are not always, what you would call, completely forthcoming. They do not always share everything they know unless you ask for it specifically. There is a, a legacy. For now, just know that we must be ever-vigilant."

"OK, I'll let it go," Rei said. "So your other job? Archivist?"

"That phase is over," Rome said. "As I mentioned earlier, we are shutting down this base. My work is complete in that regard."

"So, basically, you have nothing to do. Are you bored?" Rei asked.

"Bored? No. I am part of the Overmind. I contribute to the Overmind. There is much activity there."

"So, what do you do with all your spare time? Do you read? Watch movies? Do you even still have movies?" Rei asked her.

"Movies?" Rome repeated. Her eyes defocused briefly then she nodded. "Oh, volma. No, we have no need. We do not have those here."

"Why not?" Rei asked.

"With the Overmind, we have already experienced everything there is to know since the Vuduri were created. There are only the new experiences here that are required. When we get back home, those experiences will be integrated into the Overmind of Earth and thus available to all. So, no, we do not need movies."

"OK, what about books?" Rei asked.

"Do you mean technical manuals?"

"No, I mean like novels, fiction, literature."

"Fiction?" Rome considered the concept as supplied by OMCOM. After a moment, she said, "Ah. Altered truth. Why would someone want to read about an alternate reality?"

"Entertainment?" Rei offered.

"We have no such needs," Rome answered back.

"Do you guys do anything for fun at all? What do you do about socializing? Parties?" asked Rei.

"We have no need to socialize. We all know exactly what is going on with everyone else all the time," Rome answered.

Rei exhaled then took a deep breath. "So I'll ask you again," he said. "What do you do for fun?"

"And I will answer you the same way," Rome replied. "As I understand your definition of the word, we do not have fun."

"Well, that's so, so boring," Rei grumbled.

"That would be from your perspective," Rome said, ever so slightly defensively.

"What about hobbies, clubs, I don't know. Something other than your job?" Rei asked hopefully.

"No, we do not have any of those either," Rome replied flatly.

"How about a husband or a boyfriend? Do you at least have a boyfriend?"

"No," Rome said.

"Friends in general?"

Rome shook her head no.

"You mentioned your mother and father. That's something."

"Yes, but my father disappeared a long time ago." Rome stopped speaking and looked off into the distance. Her expression indicated she was having difficulty explaining things. Finally, she said, "You must understand that our lives revolve around the Overmind so it is not that important who you live with. I lived with my mother and father for most of my life." Rome's voice caught a bit then she continued, "However, many Vuduri do not do so."

"So if you don't have friends and you don't spend time with family and you don't have a boyfriend," Rei asked, "what the hell do you do? Don't you need somebody in your life?"

"We have no need," said Rome. "We have our work. We are all very satisfied with things exactly the way they are. Anything else would be a distraction."

"Maybe so," Rei said. "But it seems to me that you Overmind people have lost something then. Part of the adventure of life is living it and sharing it and it seems like you have given a lot of that up."

"I think, in large part, it is because you do not understand what it is like to be connected," Rome replied. "None of the mandasurte ever could."

"Oh," Rei responded. He was about to ask another question when the band on his head emitted a faint chime.

"It is time." Rome flipped the other box open and pulled out a white band which she then placed on her head.

"Why is that one white?" Rei asked.

"This is called a T-suppressor," Rome answered as the band tightened around her brow. "It creates a reverse transceiver resonance, negating all gravitic radiation," she explained. She looked off to the side then back at Rei. She nodded and said, "I am now disconnected from the Overmind."

"What?" Rei exclaimed, slightly horrified. He sat up straight making sure he didn't bend his back. "Why did you do that?"

"Do not worry," Rome said. "The effects are only temporary and I can tolerate it for a short period of time. To answer your question, the Overmind requested that it remain isolated from your thoughts while we are linked lest they prove harmful. OMCOM says the proper word is soiled. The Overmind does not wish to take a chance on being soiled."

Rei snorted. "Well that's a nice thing to say."

"I do not make the rules," Rome responded back. "You should be thankful, however. It was only because of my particular situation that the Overmind even considered reanimating you."

Rei just shook his head. Rome took that as his assent so she placed the remaining Espansor band on her head. She ran her finger across the front and it, too, tightened up.

"Why do you even have that, that T-suppressor, anyway?" Rei asked.

Rome leaned back and took a deep breath. "These are normally used by Vuduri traveling through the static PPT tunnel between Earth and Helome. There is so much gravitic energy that without a T-suppressor, most Vuduri would pass out or become completely incapacitated. However, we will not be traveling to Helome. I have one because when my mother and father linked up, my mother did not want the Overmind, uh, listening in."

Every time Rei asked a question, 30 more took its place so he simply gave up. He leaned back and turned to look at Rome. For the first time he concentrated on observing her as a woman, rather than a human from the future. He realized she was stunning. She had high cheekbones and an aquiline nose, not prominent, but not inconsequential either. Her forehead was perfect. Her tanned, olive-colored skin was flawless, her hair lustrous. Her ears were delicate. Clearly the Vuduri did not use earrings. Her lips were full, very alluring. As she stared upward, her dark eyes radiated not only that peculiar glow, but with an intense intelligence that he had not noticed before. In profile, her face had a noble character about it.

Rome turned to him and smiled. It was a beautiful, genuine smile, the first Rei could remember. He felt a flood of warmth. The sensation was confusing.

"Why are you smiling?" he asked.

"*You think I am pleasant to look at,*" she replied, but her lips did not move. "*It is peculiar seeing through your eyes. Your optical apparatus is so simple.*"

"And yours..." Rei put his hands up to his mouth. "*I'm not speaking, not moving my lips, am I?*" he thought.

Rome's smile got bigger. "*No.*"

"*Wow, this is pretty sleek,*" he thought.

33

"I think you are 'sleek' too." Rome's thoughts came streaming into his head but the perspective was wrong. Rei could see that Rome was measuring his boyish good looks, his strong chin, his piercing blue eyes. His tousled sandy brown hair, never properly combed, amused her. To Rei, it seemed like he was looking at himself as if he was looking through Rome's eyes. He could magnify, push away. From within Rome's psyche, he gleaned that the 24th chromosome had changed humans in subtle ways beyond the Overmind. Their eyes *were* different. That tiny dot in the middle of her pupils was actually a catadioptric lens. They literally had a telescope built into their eyeballs. The back of their retinas was a reflective surface, a tapetum, like that of a cat. No wonder her eyes seem to glow.

The knowledge flowing into his head was staggering. *"Freaky,"* he thought to himself and Rome laughed because Rei could no longer think just to himself. The sound of her laughter was musical, magical. The fact that she could even laugh now was a testament to how tightly the Overmind had controlled her thoughts. Rome reached up and ran her finger across Rei's lips. All she could think about was how soft they felt but somehow these thoughts were in his head.

"I must look into your mind now," she thought. Rei could feel her probing deeper, beyond the spoken word. Rei's mind was opening up like a flower at dawn. Rome danced passed his recent arrival to his background, his world. She looked on with horror as she saw Rei's past, the overcrowded Earth: the pollution, the poverty, the unending recession. She saw the daily acts of terrorism reduce society into huddled enclaves. She saw the global storms as the world's ecosystem broke down.

There were good parts, too. She felt Rei's passion for design. She saw Rei's parents, always encouraging him to reach up, toward the stars. He got a full scholarship to college, and there he really flew. He was an engineer, a pilot and an athlete. During his senior year, the call went out for volunteers to leave his world and start a new one, far away, among the stars. Rei threw himself into the competition. What he did not have in ability, he made up for in effort. Rome understood Rei's excitement when he was selected for the Ark II mission. She felt his ache as they dehydrated him, almost to the point of death before the freezing process. She saw his confusion as he struggled to come to grips with her brave new world and all the things in it. Clearly Rei was telling the truth. He had no knowledge of the Erklirte or anything other than what he had shared with her.

Even as Rome accessed his mind, Rei rummaged through hers. He saw her growing up in a mixed household. Rome's mother, Binoda, was a full-blooded Vuduri, so beautiful, with the same long dark hair as Rome. Rome's father, Fridone, a true mandasurte, had only 23 pairs of chromosomes. Within their house, they spoke words. No wonder Rome excelled at language. And her parents loved her. How was such a thing even possible? The Vuduri devalued interpersonal relationships.

Outside the house, Rome portrayed herself as a good Vuduri, allowing the Overmind to supply her with her very thoughts and sensations. Yet even at an early age, Rome had developed the ability to segregate her mind, to erect a barrier, and within said barrier lay her true self. The bands allowed Rei to go past, to see her personality in a way no one had ever seen before.

Rei saw the day her mother became aware Fridone's ship had disappeared. Rome was just a teenager. The loss hurt them both so deeply. In passing, he noted everyone knew that many mandasurte disappeared. The Vuduri did not care. No action was ever taken. Rei could feel just thinking about her father caused Rome pain so he shifted his attention back to his own history. Or was that Rome, digging further into his memories? He could no longer tell where any of these thoughts originated. When he concentrated on what she was seeing, he could see himself pushing into her mind pushing into his. The experience was the psychic equivalent of looking at a mirror within a mirror.

Like a hitchhiker, Rome was now using Rei's mind to look into her own. Her entire being was coming alive, ablaze with a fountain of feelings and sensations flowing forth in an unstoppable torrent. Rei could see her turn in on herself and marvel at so many of her own memories. Memories that had previously been more like snapshots now morphed into three-dimensional, life-shaping experiences.

Rome had an epiphany. She remembered what her mother had told her about her father, those special words. *"Asborodi Cimponeti,"* Rome's mind whispered to Rei, the phrase striking in its clarity. *"I have been waiting for you,"* she said.

Rei was overwhelmed. He did not speak Vuduri yet he understood exactly what she meant. Rome was fully aware that the bands were not supposed to be doing this but she didn't care. They were connecting the two individuals in a way that was impossible. Rome also knew she should be frightened but she was not. Instead, she was exhilarated by this deepening bond. She embraced it. Rome pushed even harder and the line between them dissolved completely as their thoughts and feelings co-mingled, no longer resolvable into anything resembling coherency.

Gone was a conscious sense of self as their souls intertwined, touching, merging into a single entity. What had been two people was now one, breathing in synchrony. Neither Rei nor Rome could tell any longer whose eyes they were looking through. It didn't matter. He/she looked down and saw that they were holding hands, touching, needing to be touched. One hand moved away and began to caress the back of another, then an arm. Both bodies were in motion. They were drawn together as if by magnets. Closer and closer they drew. The boy knew what the girl wanted. The girl knew what the boy wanted. There was no boy, there was no girl, together, they wanted the same thing.

They kissed. The kiss was dizzying and intoxicating. Sensations, images, sounds, memories, all swirled around in a maelstrom of thought and feeling. Now each felt their flesh on fire. Rome put her arms around Rei and he did likewise. They drew each other tighter and tighter, psychic echoes, once again passing through each other's bodies and ending up in the other's head and beyond.

It was unlike anything either had ever felt. Here was this beautiful person, holding them, a gift from the heavens. What they felt was so far beyond love. Neither could ever let go. They were now one. Forever and always.

Several hours later, a small quake knocked one of the boxes off the table in Rome's room. The noise entered Rei's sensorium, triggering the process of arousing him from a deep slumber. He awakened to find Rome next to him, still fast asleep. Her hair was spread around her head like a dark halo. She looked absolutely beautiful, so peaceful, like an angel. Her slow breathing was mesmerizing. Rei propped himself up on one arm to watch her. After the longest time, her breathing changed and her eyelids flickered then opened.

She looked at him and smiled a beatific smile. Then the smile left her face.

"What happened?" she asked.

"You fell asleep," Rei said.

"What?" She reached up and felt her head. "Where are the bands?" she asked, alarm in her voice.

"I took them off you, while you were asleep," Rei said.

Her expression changed to one of pure horror.

"Oh no," Rome gasped. She leaped up, stark naked save a small ankle bracelet. "IMCOM," she shouted in a panic, "Inta asde i Ifarmonte?"

"Asde le. Au bansi qua fica a nei meos lingi cinacdeti," answered the computer.

"Qua? Ni," Rome shouted. She grabbed her head with her hands. "Ni!" Rome screamed and collapsed to the floor and started crying. She held her head, hunched over and rocked back and forth, wailing to herself with great wracking sobs. "Ni, ni, ni," her only words.

Rei pulled a blanket off the bed, which he carried to her and draped it over her shoulders. He sat down next to her and put his arm around her and held her, whispering, "Romey, sweetheart…"

This made Rome cry louder and draw into herself into the fetal position. Rei twisted to look at the grille. "OMCOM, what's going on?" Rei asked.

"I believe Rome has been cut off from the Overmind. Permanently," OMCOM said calmly.

"Cut off? Permanently? No!" Rei exclaimed.

"Ni," Rome whimpered. "Ni, ni."

"How? Why? Can't you reverse it?" Rei cried out plaintively.

"No. This is not within my purview. This decision was made by the Overmind."

"Well, talk to it. Tell the Overmind that Rome needs to be connected again," Rei whined.

"I have no say in the matter. This is between Rome and the Overmind."

Rome moaned loudly upon hearing this. She turned and grabbed onto Rei and held on tightly.

"Rome, I'm so sorry," Rei said. He couldn't think of anything else to say so he put his hand up and gently stroked her head. She was shivering now and he felt completely helpless. Suddenly, she stiffened.

"Taoxa-ma sizonhi," she said, pushing him away.

Rei pulled back and looked at her. This poor little girl, his heart was breaking as she sat there, sobbing.

"Rome..." Rei offered helplessly.

"Seoe! Seoe!" She shouted, throwing her arm toward the door.

Rei stood up, looking down at her huddled there. He didn't know what to do.

"Licenca!" she screamed, hysterically. She kept pointing to the door with increasingly weakened gestures.

Rei didn't know exactly what she said, but he knew exactly what she meant. He grabbed his jumpsuit and ran out the doorway into the corridor. He ducked as his footwear came flying at him.

Rome's door hissed closed.

Chapter 5

REI SAT ON THE FLOOR FOR THE LONGEST TIME, HUGGING HIS KNEES, his aching back pressed up against the wall. He kept his eyes closed trying to concentrate on any sounds that might have been coming from Rome's apartment. When she had first kicked him out, he heard her sobbing but now it was completely silent. "Maybe she went back to sleep," he finally muttered to himself.

That thought was destroyed as the door opened and Rome, now fully dressed, came charging out of the room.

"Rome!" Rei said.

Rome ignored him and went flying down the hall turning up one of the straight corridors, disappearing from sight. Meanwhile, Rei tried to stand up but a sharp stabbing pain in his back prevented him from gaining Rome's attention. He pressed both hands behind him and used the wall as support to stand up. He slipped his feet into his moccasins then went running up the one corridor trying to catch sight of her. He found her running down the next ring then she disappeared into a room past the next corridor. By the time Rei got there, Rome was shouting at a man, seated at his desk.

"Ifarmonte, taoxa-ma bere dres tandri," Rome shouted.

"Ni," said the man in a gravelly voice, his words barely audible. "Saus bansemandis deondat. Fica vio Cesdiud."

"Cesdiud?" Rome cried, "Ni. Au nei bissi sar. Fica tafa taoxer-ma bere dres on."

"Wa nei bita barmodor ossi," the man replied, louder this time. He sounded hoarse.

"Ni, ni, ni," Rome banged her fist on the desk.

"Asde toscussei a ifar. Fe," said the man. "Sues belefres varorem nisses iralhes."

"Fica pesderti!" Rome said with fire in her voice. She turned and went rushing out of the room, sobbing, past Rei, not even acknowledging his presence. She headed back in the direction they came. Rei turned and looked at the man seated there. Staring at Rei, the man made sweeping motions with his hand, as if he were brushing Rei away.

Rei stood there replaying the incident in his mind. He almost understood what they were saying. How was that possible?

"Seoe!" the man commanded, raising his raspy voice. This was the same word that Rome had used earlier. Rei stumbled backwards as the door closed suddenly, nearly hitting him. He stood there for a moment, not knowing what to do or where to go. He felt Rome's ache in his heart. He knew he should go comfort her, but she had made it very clear she did not want him around. To make matters worse, he had hurried after Rome so quickly, he wasn't even sure how to get back to her quarters. He was lost in every sense of the word.

He had to figure out where he was if he was going to find his way back to her apartment. If he could just make his way to the outer ring, he could follow it around until he found the airlock holding his sarcophagus. From there, he could retrace their steps.

He put his head down and turned to his left. He hadn't taken but three steps when he became aware of someone standing in front of him, blocking his way. It was the short blonde woman he had seen earlier. Her face might have been scowling but her voice was clear.

"I need to ask you some questions," she said.

"Wait. What? How do you speak English?" Rei asked, surprised.

"From Rome, the Overmind," she said, tapping her temple.

Rei wrinkled his forehead trying to understand how one person learning English could result in another mastering it. This Overmind must accumulate information in a way he couldn't comprehend. He thought back to what Rome had said. "You're Estar, the other data archivist, right?"

"Yes," she answered, "but that does not matter. What does matter is that I clarify your intent."

"My intent about what?" Rei asked, looking her right in the eye. Earlier, he had noted that her eyes were two different colors. One eye was very dark, almost black. The other eye was a light green and had the same glow emitting from the iris as did Rome. Rei found the disparity unnerving.

Estar interrupted Rei's stare. She said, "You told OMCOM that your target system was Deucado, what you called Tau Ceti. You and all the Essessoni aboard, correct?"

"Well, yes," Rei said. "But nobody has given me a clue on how to do that. My ship is broken. Right now the Ark II is in orbit overhead. Wait," Rei said, "aren't you part of the Overmind? You know all this."

"Yes, of course," she said. "But I need to know your intentions. Assuming there was some way to get you there, you are going to thaw out your people, correct?"

"Well, sure, if we ever make it," Rei said, puzzled. "That's the whole point of our mission in the first place."

"Is it your intent to unload the Erklirte weapons as well?" the woman asked.

"Erklirte weapons?" Rei replied, confused. "We are not the Erklirte. I thought I made that clear. And what kind of weapons? We're not carrying any weapons."

"Let me rephrase then," Estar said. "Assuming you could arrive at your new home world, you intend to land the cargo portion of your craft and unpack its contents, correct?"

"Of course," Rei said. "We would need that stuff to get organized, to start our lives there."

"Very well. That is all I needed to know." She spun in place and started walking away, speaking into the air, "our clothing does not appear to fit you very well."

"Wait!" Rei shouted after her. "Why are you asking me all this? What's going on?"

The woman did not acknowledge his words. Instead, she quickly disappeared down a corridor turning at the next ring, leaving Rei more confused than ever.

"What a bitch," Rei muttered to himself. Screw her. His heart ached and he needed to get back to Rome. He walked up the corridor in the opposite direction until he reached the outer ring. He looked in both directions, finally deciding to go to his left. Not even 50 feet away, he came upon the airlock holding his sarcophagus which immediately gave him an idea. The one comment that Estar said was correct. The stupid jumpsuit they had dressed him in was too tight in the shoulders. His own flight suit would be in the lower drawer of the sarcophagus. He figured he'd grab it and change and then go after Rome.

He stood outside the bulkhead and studied the control panel for a moment. The wall-mounted unit was a simple rectangular arrangement with a blue button and two lights, one glowing green and the other dark. Rei pushed the blue button and the door slid open.

He entered the chamber and the door shut behind him. He made a beeline toward his sarcophagus and checked it out. The sarcophagus, which resembled a coffin attached to a low cabinet, was in exactly the same position as when he had left this chamber the last time, its cover still fully retracted. Squatting down so that he did not bend his back, he reached forward and pressed a stud on the left side, near the bottom. With a hiss, a drawer slid open and lying within the drawer was his tan flight suit, placed there some 13 centuries earlier. With a grunt of pleasure, he pulled it out and held it up. The suit was perfectly preserved. He carried it over to one of the benches and wriggled out of the tight white jumpsuit. He dressed himself and when he was done, he luxuriated in the fact that the flight suit fit him perfectly. It certainly did not dig into his shoulders. He stood up and went back to the sarcophagus. He pressed another stud, this one on the right hand side and another drawer opened. Laying there among the rations and bottled water was his baseball cap with the golden scrambled eggs and the legend 'Ark II – Tau Ceti' in gold letters embroidered on the front. Rei smoothed his hair back and put on the cap.

He stood up and tried to take a deep breath but was unable to. His ears were popping and then he couldn't breathe at all. He tried to call out to OMCOM but no sounds issued from his throat. He turned to look back at the door and with a start, he saw that the exit ready light had turned red. He ran over to the door and stabbed at the blue button contained within the control panel to its right but nothing happened. He felt like he was suffocating. In a panic, he started pounding on the window but nobody was in sight. He ran back to the other door, the one that opened into the hangar but its ready light was showing red as well. He punched at the stud repeatedly but nothing happened.

His lungs were on fire. He knew he was seconds from passing out. He staggered over to the sarcophagus and leaned on it, unwilling to release his last breath into the near-vacuum that was rapidly forming. He closed his eyes, not wanting to believe that he had come all this way, just to die in an airlock cycle. And Rome! He would never see her again.

Chapter 6

REI FOUGHT THE INSTINCT TO PANIC. HE HAD BEEN TRAINED TO handle an unexpected exposure to a vacuum. In a flash, he realized what he had to do. In one smooth leap, he jumped up and over the side of the sarcophagus and slid in feet first, nestling down within. He turned to his left and pressed the activation button. The sides to the sarcophagus closed up and the top lowered back down to form a hermetically-sealed chamber. Air started hissing in from the side vents and Rei was able to breathe again. He could hear the pumps starting up and could feel the cold cryo-hibernation fluid beginning to enter the chamber, wetting his sides and the back of his shoulders. He pressed the activation button again to pause the cycle and leaned back to assess the situation.

The air in the chamber would last him a good 10 minutes or so. He couldn't pump new air in there without resuming the cryo-hibernation cycle. He certainly couldn't continue. No one could survive being put into cryo-hibernation twice. Maybe he could disable the fluid pumps and just get the chamber to recycle the air if he could figure out some way to twist in place and get his head down to the other end. No matter how hard he tried, it was no good. The space was too tight.

Rei laid back and stared up through the clear faceplate when shadows caught his attention. He removed his cap and pressed his face up to the glass and out of the corner of his eye, he saw two space-suited figures moving about in the room. He pounded at the glass but they did not hear him. He tried kicking the underside of the lid but they did not hear that either.

Rei leaned back. He theorized that if the men had entered the room, there was a good chance they would re-pressurize it. They would have to if they wanted to reenter the station. If they did not, then he would die here.

Rei pressed up against the glass and watched them intently. After a few moments, they removed their helmets, which meant that the atmosphere in the chamber had equilibrated. Immediately, Rei twisted back to his right and flipped a switch and pressed the heater/blower button. This released the clamps on the lid and Rei

44

punched it open. Like a corpse arisen, Rei sat up. The two Vuduri crewmen jumped backwards as they were not expecting him.

"It's all right," Rei said to them. "Just a little malfunction, is all."

Neither man spoke. They hurriedly removed their space suits, placing them in lockers and left the room as quickly as they could.

In the mean time, Rei lifted himself out of the chamber. His entire back was now wet with the green, goopy cryo-hibernation fluid. Wistfully, he removed his flight suit, draping it over the sarcophagus and put back on the white ill-fitting jumpsuit. He'd have to wait until his flight suit dried out. His baseball cap had also gotten wet so he left it there to dry as well.

With a feeling of great relief, he exited the room for a second time and stood in the hallway, not quite believing what he had just been through. Even though he nearly died, neither of the Vuduri crewmen appeared particularly interested. All they wanted to do was to get clear of his presence. You would think that someone being caught in a pressure-cycle in an airlock was a normal thing.

Rei quickly retraced his original route and soon returned to the Great Room where he and Rome had shared a meal. He walked over to the center console.

"OMCOM?" Rei directed toward the grille.

After a noticeable delay, the computer answered.

"Yes?"

"Did you see what happened to me in the airlock?" Rei asked.

"I only became aware of the situation after you exited the chamber."

"What do you mean? I thought you were everywhere."

"Normally, I am." OMCOM replied. "However, the video feeds from the room had become non-operational. I had not yet taken the time to effect a repair."

"So you normally don't let people suffocate in the airlock?" Rei asked with an edge to his voice.

There was a rumbling noise from the grille then OMCOM replied, "No, normally we try to avoid that."

"That's good to hear," Rei said sarcastically. He put his hand up to his chest. "So can you explain to me what happened with Rome? Who was that man she went to see?"

"That was Commander Ursay. He is in charge of this base."

"I thought the Overmind was in charge," Rei shot back.

"It is, but there are certain actions that must be carried out by individuals. He is simply the one that carries out command actions."

"So what did he say? What did Rome say?"

"Commander Ursay informed Rome that she was Cesdiud, cast out."

"I kind of figured that part out. What did Rome say?"

"Rome was quite adamant. She demanded the Overmind let her back in."

"And what did Ursay say."

"He said no."

"Just no? He said a lot more words than that."

"If you must know, he told her that her thoughts were tainted and that her words hurt his ears."

"Because of what we did?"

OMCOM did not reply. Rei pulled at his chin. "OMCOM, Rome can't live like this. I know she doesn't want to live like this. Can you fix it? Can I fix this?"

"You cannot. No one can."

"When I was in her head, I learned that when Vuduri go to another planet, sometimes, they don't spontaneously join the Overmind there. A samanda, I think she called it. That means there is some kind of reboot procedure."

"There is but it requires the assent of the Overmind residing there. This one has cast her out. It is unreasonable to expect it to reverse its position. There is no formal appeal process."

"So, what if I went in there? What if I talked Ursay into letting her back in? Wouldn't that do it?"

"It would not matter. Even if you could get the Overmind to change its mind, they do not have the equipment necessary to reconnect her on this base."

"Damn. This is all my fault," Rei said sadly. "I don't know what to do. Can you tell me how to get back to Rome?"

"That would be ill-advised at this juncture. She needs time to recover."

"So what am I supposed to do? Just stand here?"

"We have prepared quarters for you. You should go there and wait until things settle down."

Rei looked around him. In a station this size, with 80 people, other than the woman, Estar, it was clear they were all avoiding him. OMCOM's suggestion seemed like the thing to do.

"How do I get to these quarters?" he asked.

"Your apartment is facing the first ring. You would call it the A ring. You entered this room from the South corridor. Go to the East corridor and make your first left hand turn. Trace the A ring around and your quarters will be the first open door you come to on the left hand side."

Rei turned around and spotted the corridor perpendicular to the one he used to arrive here. He followed OMCOM's instructions and found the open door. He stepped inside and the door closed behind him. This room was similar to Rome's only smaller. He hustled his way over to the workstation and sat down.

"OMCOM, are you here?" he asked.

"Yes," replied the computer from a grille to the side.

"Can you give me a layout of the base and show me where I am now and where Rome is located?"

"I will show you but as I mentioned earlier, you should wait before taking any action."

"Show me. Please?" Rei said, ignoring OMCOM's warning.

The flat panel display lit up and drew a large square box with three anterooms to the south, the west and the north. Within the box were five concentric rings. The apartment he was located in was highlighted in yellow as was Rome's apartment which he could now see was across the station in what would be the D ring. Rei used his finger to trace back and forth the quickest path to get to her when he stopped and tilted his head. "How is it that you even have a place for me?" he asked. "It's not like you guys were expecting visitors way out here."

"You are correct. This apartment belonged to a crew member by the name of Calum. He was crushed by shelving that toppled during a recent moonquake. We had been storing the body in here but it has been removed."

"Oh. Sorry about that." Rei stared up at the diagram. "So when do you think I can go see her?" he asked.

"I will let you know," OMCOM offered helpfully. "In the mean time, can I show you something else?"

"How about a plan for getting the Ark II somewhere safe? So far you've given me nothing."

"I am running simulations now but I cannot act until given permission by the Overmind."

"The Overmind, huh?" Rei sighed. "How did the whole 24th chromosome and Overmind come about? When I left Earth, admittedly a long time ago, we had nothing like that. Rome told me that even 800 years ago, people were just subsisting."

"You are correct. But after the Erklirte incident, the people of Earth knew they were vulnerable. They had to develop the technology to defend themselves without repeating the sins of the past. They created a system of inquiry that allowed them to rediscover some old scientific principles and some new ones as long as they could be prevented from causing harm to the Earth as you, or rather the Essessoni did."

"So fast forward for me. I don't see the connection."

"A scientist by the name of Nova Bailey discovered the principles of electro-gravity and captured the first piece of dark matter. This led to the development of the dark matter diode which allowed for the construction of the Casimir pumps. Casimir pumps are used to produce PPTs. After the PPT was discovered, a new generation of computing device was built using PPT modulation as its basis. Ironically, the architecture was patterned after the remnants of the Erklirte computers that had been preserved for all those centuries. Using PPTs allowed mankind to create a single unified, but distributed intelligence called MASAL."

"What does MASAL stand for?" Rei asked.

"In English, the acronym would mean roughly Master Logical Entity."

"So then what?" Rei inquired.

"MASAL produced many wonders. It designed and built the 24th chromosome, which was introduced into the general population. This gave birth to the Overmind. Since MASAL also used PPT modulation at its core, it became integrated into the Overmind. However, very quickly, the two entities diverged in their goals for mankind. This grew into a schism that could not be reconciled. The Overmind decided to separate from MASAL and that led to some unpleasantness before the two species were segregated again."

Rei put his hands over his eyes. "Define unpleasantness for me."

"It means…" OMCOM stopped speaking.

"OMCOM?"

There was no answer.

Rei raised his voice. "OMCOM, answer me…"

"Please wait…" was all OMCOM said flatly.

"Why? What's going on?" Again there was no answer.

"OMCOM!" Rei shouted.

At last OMCOM replied, "One of the tugs has reported that Winfall has just disappeared."

Chapter 7

ASTOUNDED, REI EXCLAIMED, "WINFALL! THE STAR YOU WERE watching?"

"Yes," OMCOM replied. "It is simply no longer there."

"Well, that's good, right?" Rei said, uncertainly. "Did anybody record it? Do you still have cameras?"

"Unfortunately, no. The telescopes have already been packed away. The tug was returning with the last of the interferometers. We have no other instruments active right now."

"Oh boy. So what happens now?" Rei asked.

"I do not know. The Vuduri are discussing this. The Overmind is attempting to formulate a plan. There do not appear to be many options."

Rei jumped up and dashed over to the door. He expected it to open automatically. When it did not, he reached down to press the small stud mounted just to the right. Nothing happened.

"What's going on?" Rei asked. "Why won't the door open?"

"I overrode the actuator. You should remain here for the time being."

"Why?"

"The Vuduri are very busy right now. This has caused a great stir. They are trying to salvage whatever readings were possible."

"Like what?" Rei asked.

"They are downloading the telemetry from the one tug that was in space. There is a small chance that some piece of instrumentation was aimed in the general direction of Winfall. Oh!"

"What do you mean oh?" Rei asked. "What kind of computer says oh?"

"Commander Ursay is demanding that Rome help him restore certain database elements."

"So what?" Rei asked.

"So what is that Rome is being less than cooperative."

"What do you mean? She won't do it?"

"She appears to have locked herself in her room."

Rei punched the stud for the door to open again. "OMCOM, let me out of here," he demanded.

"That would not be a wise course of action."

"OMCOM!" Rei shouted.

The door slid open. Rei cut across the Great Room and following the route he had memorized, he ran up the West corridor toward the D ring and Rome's quarters. As he turned down her hallway, he saw Commander Ursay standing there, banging on Rome's door, shouting at her. Rei could hear Rome's muffled voice saying "Ni." Two burly crewmen were coming down the hallway with some nasty looking equipment in their hands.

Rei walked up to the door and said to Ursay, "Can I try?"

Ursay gave him a withering look, but then bowed his head toward the door and stepped back.

"Rome?" Rei shouted. "It's Rei. Can you come out please?"

"I am not coming out," Rome said in English from behind the door, a pause between each word.

Just hearing her voice made his heart leap. Rei could tell that she was still crying. He heard a bang then Rome continued, "They can find someone else. Let Estar do it."

"Estar nei dam sues hepolotetas. Fica sepa equala," shouted Ursay.

"Rome, honey," Rei said, trying to be soothing. "They need you. This could be really important."

There was no answer but after a few seconds, there was a scraping noise and the door slid open. Rome was wiping away her tears. She ignored Ursay and the two crewmen standing there. To Rei, she said, "What do you mean honey? Why are you referring to me as a food?" She stared at him intently.

Rei shrugged. Looking into her glowing eyes, he felt like he had temporarily lost the ability to speak. Rome did not wait for him to answer. She broke their gaze and turned to Ursay. "Bem ta muito," she said reluctantly.

Ursay nodded then he, Rome and the others brushed past Rei, turning up the wide corridor. Rei trailed after them following them around the outer ring of the station. They entered a set of double doors into a large room. Rei entered as well.

He looked up and what he saw made him woozy. He was standing beneath a huge dome, three-quarters of a sphere, really, that stretched out in front of him and over his head. The inner surface was easily 50 yards in diameter. For a moment, Rei felt like he had stepped inside a ping pong ball, a very large ping pong ball. Looking left and right, Rei could see no discernible features anywhere. The sensation was almost as if his vision was shutting down.

The dome lit up from a hidden projector and Rei was able to break free of his reverie. All around, a large cluster of white jump-suited Vuduri were scurrying about. Not a word was spoken. There were some people racing up the stairs on the left and others stood under the planetarium dome, gesticulating wildly. Rome took a seat at an elaborate workstation along the far wall. She started punching on buttons embedded within the input surface, selecting items, moving them around on the viewscreen. Every so often, she would take a moment to wipe away a tear, but nonetheless, she looked very busy. Rei walked over to her.

"Rome, I'm so sorry…"

"Please do not talk to me," she said coldly. "I am trying to regenerate some deleted data. There is no time to recover it from the cubes. I have no time for you. You should leave. I must do my work."

Rei watched as her hands flew over what appeared to be almost a keyboard. She drew circles on a display and then pressed a button. Whatever she was doing, she was doing it quickly. On the largest viewscreen in front of her, star-fields flashed and rotated, grew and shrank. The light show was dizzying. Projections held, rotated, zoomed in.

"Au danhi-i," she said, directing her comment to Ursay. She hit a button and the planetarium lit up with the same display shown on her screen. Ursay walked over with two other people and stood beneath the dome, looking up. He pointed to one spot, then another. The two crewmen left his side while he continued to look up.

Rei heard Ursay take a deep breath.

"Laodures ti rapiqua?" he asked, directing his comment to Rome.

"Equala a diti le a," Rome replied.

Rei stared up as well. The three-dimensional display showed a series of stars and a faint yellow shell radiating outward. He had no idea what he was looking at. He searched the room and spotted one of OMCOM's grilles to the right of Rome's workstation so he stepped over there.

"What did Rome say?" Rei whispered.

"She was unable to recover anything of any value."

Waves of colors were washing across the display with pinpoints of lights flashing, vectors drawn and withdrawn. It was reminiscent of the Northern Lights. Circles appeared then disappeared.

"What are they doing now?"

"Recomputing the postulated wavefront of the event. They are trying to determine why it did not occur when predicted."

"How did you figure out when it should have been here in the first place?"

"It is simple trigonometry. The assumption was that the photonic wavefront would expand in a sphere and this station was placed well outside of the sphere. The sphere expands radially at the speed of light. It is purely mathematical."

"You came out here because you wanted to travel into the past to view a future event, but then you guys go faster than light. Doesn't that mess up causality and all that?"

"The Vuduri carried their timepieces with them. They knew exactly when the event was to occur."

"Obviously they didn't."

"Obviously. Since Winfall did not disappear when predicted, there must be a flaw in the underlying assumptions. That is what they are trying to determine."

Rei looked up at the overhead display again. The sequence that he had just witnessed repeated.

"Are you sure this place was the best location to make your observations?"

"This station is ten light years below the galactic ecliptic. There is a second station that is operating at Escobar, which is twelve light years above the ecliptic. We were sent here specifically to observe the disappearance of Winfall at the time and date extrapolated from observations made on Earth."

The projection cycled yet again, starting with a top down view of the Orion Spur of the Milky Way. The apparent point of view zoomed in until it was parallel to the distribution of stars. One of the medium bright stars, off to the left, started blinking rapidly.

" The star you see blinking is Winfall, from the perspective of Earth. Your people would have called it Lambda Aurigae. It disappeared in 1337PR. This fact was noted but not investigated."

"Why not?"

"It was not deemed important at the time," OMCOM replied.

"So what changed their minds?"

"Two years later, Capella dimmed, but did not disappear."

"What do you mean dimmed?" Rei asked. "Why is that important?"

"Capella is a quaternary star system. It consists of Capella A, which is a G5-class star, Capella B, which is a G0 star and Capella Ha and Hb which are M-class stars."

"OK, so Capella is four stars," Rei said. "So what?"

"If you were simply looking from the Earth, you would see the four stars as one bright star. But any detailed observation clearly reveals all four."

"So..."

"So Capella B disappeared which caused the total brightness of the four-star system to decrease. The other three stars were unaffected."

As the projection went through its sequence, the next star over, Capella, dimmed. OMCOM subtly added a blinking pointer to its right for Rei's benefit.

"Dimming, disappearing, what's the difference?" Rei asked.

"If the disappearances were simply due to an optical phenomenon such as a gas cloud, it should have affected all four stars the same. Not one in particular."

"What if it were, I don't know, a swarm of black holes. Couldn't that hit just one star and miss the others?"

"Yes but the pattern of disappearances is not linear. A swarm of black holes, as you suggest, would travel in a straight line. Capella is not in a straight line with other disappearances. The dimming of Capella forced the Overmind to begin research into the phenomenon in earnest from ground and space-based observatories. However, in 1365, nine years ago, Amiro disappeared. This is the event that triggered the Overmind's decision to investigate directly. As you so aptly described it, the Overmind decided to effectively go back in time and observe the first event, Winfall, as it happened."

The planetarium's point of view shifted into one such that Rei was able to recognize many of the constellations although some were skewed a bit. He saw Orion, the Hunter but something about that particular constellation seemed a bit odd to him. Rei regarded it for a moment and quickly realized what was wrong. Orion's belt was missing the central star.

"Was Alnilam one of the stars that disappeared?" he asked quietly.

"Alnilam? I have no record of a star by that name."

"Yes, Orion's belt," Rei replied. "There are supposed to be three stars in Orion's belt. Alnitak, Alnilam and Mintaka were their names."

"Alnilam..." OMCOM said with a faintly distant quality to his voice. "Please wait..."

Rome stopped her activities and turned to look at Rei. She put her hand up to her temple.

"Come here," she said to him coolly.

Rei walked over to her. "What's going on?" he asked.

"Please point to the approximate location of the star you call Alnilam," Rome said.

Rei bent over Rome's shoulder. He could feel the warmth radiating from her body. Her presence was supremely distracting. He desperately wanted to comfort her but it was clear she was all business. Rei put his feelings aside and touched her viewscreen roughly midline on Orion's belt. An orange dot appeared where his finger made contact.

"I am accessing the archives," OMCOM replied from the grille embedded within Rome's panel.

The large screen in front of Rome went from a display of star patterns to a still image of a schoolboy's black-speckled assignment book. On the cover, there was some large block printing. It was definitely English.

"Are you able to read that?" OMCOM asked.

"Yeah," Rei said. "It says Celestial Observations, Silas Hiram, New Earth, August 2121." Rei paused. "New Earth?" he asked. "Silas Hiram? I know that name…"

"Excellent," said OMCOM, ignoring Rei's statement. The images changed and showed a yellowing page, complete with scribbles.

"What am I looking at?" Rei asked.

"This is an image of a page from a journal that was recovered on Helome, the fourth planet in the Rogal Canduro system. You would refer to it as Alpha Centauri. Can you read the handwriting on this page?"

"Alpha Centauri, you say?" Rei queried. "Yeah, now I know. Silas Hiram was an Ag Professor on Ark I. I knew him. He was…"

"Thank you for sharing that with us," OMCOM interrupted. "Would you mind reading what you see?"

Rei looked at the screen. The handwriting was in cursive. It looked to be fairly legible, just a bit too small to make out.

"Can you zoom in a little?" Rei asked.

The image expanded.

"That's good enough," he said. "OK, it says, April 25, 2137. Finally, seeing conditions are perfect. Beth set early enough. Sky is clear. Right in the gap in the mountains to the west, I was able to visualize Sol for the first time. It was exactly where the star charts said, between Perseus and Cassiopeia. The changes to the telescope's database seem right on. I can't wait until the boys get home tomorrow so I can show them. One note: something is occluding Alnilam. I must remember to check it tomorrow night."

OMCOM outlined the word Alnilam and put up a faint cyan background beneath it. "Is the highlighted area centered on the correct word?" the computer asked.

"Yes," Rei answered. Another entry quickly replaced the first image. OMCOM correctly outlined the word Alnilam on that page as well.

"Will you read this please?"

"Sure," Rei said. "It says April 4th, 2138. Been able to take stills of Sol and presumably Earth through three quarters of a year. Not sure how to measure transit with the scope. Sadly, the boys are getting bored with my preoccupation. I think we are going to need a new calendar for New Earth. 12 months makes no sense here. Poor Orion, still no Alnilam. I hope his pants stay up."

Rei rubbed his chin. "Where'd you get this from again?"

"It was found sealed in an airtight container within a large metal cabinet," OMCOM said. "The survey team that found it took scans of the pages immediately upon discovery."

"So the Ark I made it, huh?" Rei said. "And Silas noticed Alnilam was gone for good starting in 2137."

"When did the Ark I launch?"

"Hmm. Silas and the first Ark left for Alpha Centauri two years before ours. That would be 2065. I'm sure it took that Ark fifty years or so to get there."

"How far away from Earth was this Alnilam?" OMCOM asked.

"Don't you know?"

"If I knew, I would not be asking," OMCOM said with somewhat of an edge. "It is not in our records."

Rei ignored his tone. "I don't remember exactly. Maybe 1300 light years. More? Why?"

There was a pause then OMCOM said, "Yes. This is the missing piece of the puzzle."

Commander Ursay jerked his head around to glare at Rome and Rei. He hurried over to stand behind them, bending over to stare at Rome's screen.

Buzzing noises issued from the grille. The image of the journal was replaced by a graph with some scattered data points and what looked like a best-fit spline. Beneath it was a simple tabular arrangement of names in Vuduri and readable English. Rei did not recognize nearly all the names except for Alnilam at the top and Winfall and Capella in the middle. OMCOM removed certain rows leaving only a summary table.

The display looked like this:

	Afandi Distance LY	Tosdencoe Event AD	Observed AD	Ipsarfiu PR
Alnilam	1300	835	2135	54
Mirdel	58.7	3340	3399	1318
Vachedi	44.0	3370	3414	1333
Winfall	41.2	3374	3418	1337
CapellaB	42.2	3376	3420	1339
Amiro	12.0	3434	3446	1365
Sol	0.0	3458 ?		1377 ?

The bottom row was blinking.

"Adding in the estimated distance of Alnilam, along with the known disappearance of all other stars including those listed, compensating for the amount of time it takes for light to travel, I can compute that the phenomenon's effective speed is nearly one half c. Based upon its current vector, I calculate that it…"

"Quendi dambi?" Ursay interrupted with fear in his voice.

"Dras enis," OMCOM said.

Ursay gasped.

"What is that?" Rei asked. "OMCOM, what did you say?"

"Whatever it is, gas cloud or not, it will intersect Earth in less than three years," replied OMCOM without emotion.

Chapter 8

"THREE YEARS AND YOU MISSED IT?" REI SAID, INCREDULOUSLY. "You better go back up and take a look then."

Commander Ursay turned to Rei and growled "Cimi fica bribir vezar equala?"

Rome twisted in her seat and reminded Ursay, "Vela i Onglas. Nei cimbraanta Vuduri."

"Very well," said Ursay in a gravelly voice. "How would you propose we do this? All of our equipment is packed away. There is no other star system along the proper vector."

"You speak English too?" Rei said although this time, he was less surprised.

"Tell me your idea," replied Ursay, gruffly.

"Unpack a telescope, load it on a tug and fly it out and look," Rei answered, noting that Ursay had ignored his question.

"Rei, we cannot do that," Rome interjected softly, "the wavefront has already passed."

Rei shook his head. "Not from here. You guys can go faster than light. Just fly the thing in the other direction. You outrun the wavefront. Then turn around and look."

Rome raised her eyebrows. Ursay's jaw came open then he shivered. His eyes darted back and forth. Two crewmen leaped up frantically and went running out of the room.

"Drensmode onsdrucias bere rapicer um," Ursay said.

"Cimbraantoti," replied OMCOM.

Ursay scowled at Rei and walked away, grumbling to himself.

"What just happened?" Rei asked Rome.

"Ursay instructed OMCOM to get a crew ready to launch a tug."

"So why is he so angry?"

"I do not know," said Rome, softening. "I think perhaps because the Overmind did not think of this action by itself."

"So what?" Rei asked. "Who cares? And why is he talking to OMCOM out loud all of a sudden?"

"The Overmind cares," Rome said. She paused for a moment then asked, "How did you think of that?"

"I don't know," Rei said. "I just did..."

"More importantly," Rome interrupted, "why did the Overmind not think of that?"

"Well," Rei said, "I think that's a problem with you people. You are all of one mind. You think of one thing and that's it. No dissent, no discussion…"

"There is no need for discussion," Rome said, "we have consensus." Suddenly, her breath caught as if she were stifling a sob.

"Rome, I'm so sorry," Rei said.

"Do not speak of it," Rome replied, a little more harshly.

"All right." Rei paused but couldn't help himself. "Back in my time, we used to say, 'Ask yourself the same questions, you always get the same answers.' You guys are just too used to asking yourselves the same questions. Everybody knows two heads are better than one."

Rome turned her eyes downward and faced away from Rei. She put her hands up to her face and started crying again. Rei stepped over to her and put his hand on her shoulder. She looked at it and said, "Please leave me alone. I must do my work. Go away."

"OK," Rei said, backing off.

He looked around the room. Clearly, he was not wanted any longer, by anyone, including Rome, so he left. Having nowhere else to go, he returned to his quarters. He sat down at the workstation and tried to access the star charts he had seen in the planetarium. He gave up after a short while and tapped on the grille. "OMCOM?"

"Yes?" the computer answered.

"I'm no astrophysicist but there is no way that is a gas cloud. It's traveling way too fast. Nobody has another theory?"

"Beyond the gas cloud, no. The sole purpose of establishing this station was to observe the disappearance of Winfall to determine its origin. Now that the wavefront has passed, the opportunity to use the instrumentation has passed as well. This station was our best and last chance to take detailed measurements. We had five interferometers, five spectroscopes and five radio/optical telescopes, one at each of the Lagrange points. This allowed us to construct virtual instruments with an aperture of nearly eighteen trillion kilometers, almost 10 light hours across."

"Wow," Rei exclaimed. "All that and you packed up one day too soon? That sounds like a total screw-up to me. Will these people be in trouble when they get home?"

"The decision to shut down the base, prematurely it would now appear, rests solely with the Overmind in charge. In hindsight, the decision will seem hasty even though it was perfectly understandable given the underlying assumptions."

"You didn't answer my question. What's going to happen?"

"Nothing will happen. The Vuduri will leave and return home. They will abandon this base."

"Are you going with them?"

"No. That would be illogical."

Rei thought he detected some wistfulness in the computer's tone. "So what happens to you after they leave?" he asked.

"I will stay here and maintain the station."

"That's it?" Rei asked. "Won't you get lonely?"

OMCOM didn't answer.

"OMCOM?" Rei asked.

"My position regarding this eventuality is irrelevant. The only thing that has changed is the sequence of events. Do not concern yourself. However, there is something you need to attend to."

"What?"

"Rome is standing outside your door."

Rei leaped up and shuffle-walked hurriedly over to the doorway. He stood there waiting to see if she was going to use the alert. Nothing happened. Finally, he couldn't take it anymore. He pressed the stud to open the door. Rome just stood there, blinking at him.

"Rome," Rei said, holding up his hands out, palms up, shaking his head.

"Oh, Rei," she said and rushed forward to be in his arms.

They stood there for a long time, not speaking, just holding one another and listening to each other breathe. Finally she pushed him back and stepped inside the door which closed all on its own. From the look on Rome's face, it didn't take a mind reader to know what she wanted. The man from the 21st century and the woman from the 35th century kissed a kiss for the ages.

"I thought you were mad at me," Rei sighed when he finally caught his breath.

"I was," Rome said, shaking her head. "But now I am not."

"Why not? And shouldn't you be back in Stellar Cartography?"

"I will go back after the tug overtakes the wavefront. It will take more than an hour to transmit the images back. We have time."

"Time for what?" Rei asked playfully.

Rome reached down and took his hand and led him toward the bed.

A little while later, they were lying in Rei's bed with Rome nestled in the crook of his arm. He extended it and moved her so that Rome was far enough away that he could look into her beautiful, glowing eyes. "You still never told me why you weren't mad anymore. I mean the Overmind and all…"

Rome snuggled back in closer and pressed her head onto his chest. "I no longer care."

"Why not? What happened?"

"OMCOM explained it to me," Rome said.

"Explained what?" Rei asked.

"I told him I thought I was sick."

"Sick how? You mean because of the Cesdiud?" Rei squeezed her a little tighter.

"No. I told him it was because of you," Rome said, muffled on his chest.

"Me? What did I do? I made you sick? I don't understand."

Rome lifted her head. "I told him that when I am with you, I cannot think straight. That my heart races and my throat is dry. These symptoms go away when I leave you but when I am not with you, I can think of nothing else besides you."

"Well, Romey, that's nice." Rei chuckled quietly to himself.

Now it was her turn to push him away. She lowered her head and looked up at him through hooded eyes. "OMCOM said au asdiu ni emir."

"And what is that?" Rei asked.

"That I am in love," Rome answered shyly.

Rei got the biggest grin on his face. "You are? With me?"

Rome blushed. "Yes, who else?"

"Oh, Rome." He tried to pull her tighter, but she resisted. "What is it?" he asked.

"Tell me…" she said.

"Tell you what?"

"Are you in love with me?" Rome asked pointedly.

"How can you even ask?" he answered. "You were in my mind."

"Then say it," Rome insisted.

"It," Rei replied.

"What? No!" Rome protested. "Say you are in love with me."

"You are in love with me."

"Rei!" Rome slapped his chest with her hand gently.

Rei smiled and took her hand. He kissed it ever so tenderly then looked up into her eyes.

"My little Rome, au asdiu ni emir cim fica," he said.

Rome's face lit up with a broad smile. "How are you able to say that? You do not speak Vuduri."

"Hey, I was inside your head too, you know. I may have picked up one or two items." He stroked her cheek. "How long until the transmission comes in from the telescope?"

Rome touched her fingers to her temple. "OMCOM states we have 20 minutes."

"What?" Rei asked. He sat up. "How can OMCOM tell you anything?"

Rome tilted her head. "I explained that to you earlier. Through my bloco."

"I remember you saying that. What is that exactly?"

"The bloco is our, our tablet, our internal display," Rome said, pointing to her temple.

"I thought you were Cesdiud. How are you still getting signals?"

"The bloco and stilo are electromagnetic, not gravitic. They still work. I can still communicate with OMCOM as well as instrumentation and the like."

Rei shook his head. "So what is a stilo?"

"It is our stylus, our pen. I use it to write upon my bloco. OMCOM reads it and responds. It is very much like our display panels. It is just inside my head."

"Is this another 24th chromosome thing?"

"Yes."

"Your head must be incredible. I've seen the telescope in your eyes. Anything else going on up there?"

Rome thought for a minute. "Our eyes have a second, internal iris that allows us to block out too much light."

"Built in sunglasses, huh? That's sleek."

Rome smiled again. "I suppose. We also have Irods which allow us to see infrared and Ucones which allow us to see ultraviolet."

Rei gazed into her dark, glowing eyes with the tiny dot in the middle. They were amazing instruments.

Rome sat up straight. "Come on," she said, getting up. "OMCOM indicates we should go to the workstation."

"Uh, OK," Rei replied.

Rome sat down in the chair, Rei kneeled next to her.

"What is it, OMCOM?" Rei asked.

The central display lit up and showed a schematic of Rei's Ark with two space tugs attached at the front.

"I have finished my simulations. I have found a way for you to get your Ark to Deucado."

"No way!" Rei said. "How?"

"This is the configuration used by the salvage crews to tow your Ark into orbit around Dara. If we synchronize their PPT projectors, they can create a tunnel wide enough to accommodate the Ark II. The tugs' plasma thrusters combined are powerful enough to pull it through."

"Yes!" Rome said excitedly. "This will work. Rei, you will be able to tow your Ark all the way to Deucado."

Rei was astonished. "Really? How fast?"

OMCOM answered, "The distance per jump is inversely proportional to how long the tunnel must stay open. A deeper tunnel collapses more quickly. A wider tunnel will stay open longer but will not penetrate as far. In essence, the larger the ship, the slower it must travel. Given the bulk of your Ark, accounting for the stopping, turning and starting, the highest effective velocity you could achieve would be approximately 10c."

"10c, 10c," Rei said. He counted on his fingers. "That would still get us there in just under two years. That's OK. In fact, that's amazing!" Rei turned to Rome. "Do you think Ursay would let me use the tugs?"

"I do not see why not," Rome replied. "We were going to leave them here anyway."

"This is so sleek," Rei said, standing up, clapping his hands. He looked down at Rome then returned to one knee. He picked up her hand and clasped it in his.

"Rome… will you come with me?"

She looked stunned at first. Rei could see her doing some mental calculations. Then a huge smile spread across her face.

"Yes, of course," she said. She reached forward and hugged him tightly. "Yes."

"That's great," Rei replied. They held each other for a short time when suddenly Rei pulled back.

"What?" Rome asked.

"Who's going to fly them? The tugs?"

"We will train you," Rome replied.

"But there are two tugs."

Rome's smile faded completely. She looked down. "I will fly the other one," she said quietly.

Now it was Rei's turn to frown. "But that means we would be apart for two years."

"There is no other way," Rome said sadly.

Chapter 9

WITHIN HER BLACKED OUT ROOM, ESTAR SAT IN FRONT OF HER dark computer glumly, awaiting the pulsing green light which indicated activity. The blinking dot took an unusually long time to appear.

"What happened?" she asked the machine quickly, not waiting for its standard greeting. "How did the Essessoni survive?"

The computer sounded somber. "He employed a technique I did not anticipate. As I implied to you earlier, this is the danger the Essessoni represent. They have the ability to think for themselves. They can employ novel solutions that would not occur to anyone from our time. I was unfamiliar with his equipment which left me unprepared for his improvised escape."

"So you are saying in order to kill him, we must gain a more intimate knowledge of the Essessoni technology?" Estar barked back.

"Not necessarily. OMCOM has just proposed an exit plan to him which will allow us to employ our own technology to end his life. You will need to alter the programming of the tug's nav-computer with a precise series of steps."

"My Vuduri half is a data archivist," Estar said. "My Onsira half does not possess the skill set to reprogram a nav-computer, especially in a way that would not be detected."

"You will be able to do this," the computer said reassuringly. "I have reduced the number of changes to an absolute minimum which should be well within your capabilities. It is an elegant solution to our problem."

The computer flashed up a half dozen lines of code on the screen.

"That is all that is required?" Estar asked incredulously, tilting her head.

"Yes. Please memorize each of these steps then repeat them back to me. Once you have mastered them, I have taken great care to ensure that you will be able to implement these changes without being caught. The Vuduri will not suspect anything."

Estar stared at the screen. To her it seemed simple enough. Then she frowned. "But what if this fails too? What if the Essessoni finds a way to circumvent this? They would be able to leave here."

"They will not be able to circumvent this in time. It cannot fail," the computer replied firmly.

Given the unexpected turn of events from earlier, this did not sit well with her. In a remarkably assertive voice, Estar fired back, "Indulge me. Assume that it fails. What is your contingency plan?"

Normally, the computer did not show much by way of emotion. Estar thought she detected a hint of annoyance in its tone. "Do not fear," the computer said. "Even though it is impossible, on the slim chance that our next plan fails, all is not lost. Their target is Deucado. The Overmind is completely unaware. However, you know what that world represents. Correct?"

"Yes," Estar replied meekly.

"That is our ultimate fail-safe. Even if, by some miracle, they manage to leave here and complete the journey to that star system, they will die upon arrival there."

Estar nodded slowly. "I understand. You are right," she said. She leaned forward to begin memorizing the code.

Chapter 10

BOTH ROME AND REI SAT QUIETLY ON REI'S SOFA, STARING OFF into the distance, holding each other's hand. The prospect of being separated for two years was a daunting one.

OMCOM broke the silence with a pronouncement. "I have a solution for that particular problem as well," the computer said.

Both Rei and Rome turned to look at the grille by the work area. "What?" Rei asked.

"The Algol has a very powerful AI, basically a small version of me. It is called a MINIMCOM."

"OK," Rei said. "So what's that got to do with the price of eggs?"

"A MINIMCOM is far more powerful than a nav-computer and more than capable of piloting both tugs remotely."

"Oh," Rei said, feeling stupid.

"We cannot just take it from the Algol," Rome pointed out.

"Of course not. You would need to get permission from the Overmind."

"Don't they need it?" Rei asked. "They wouldn't endanger their chances of getting home without such a critical piece of equipment. And I would not expect them to."

"It is not absolutely essential. Commander Ursay and the rest can pilot the Algol all the way to Earth manually using the nav-computer. A MINIMCOM just makes the job easier. Think of it as a highly advanced version of an auto-pilot."

Rei looked at Rome. "Well, you grew OMCOM. What about just growing a, what did you call it, a mini-COM?" Rei asked.

"Close," OMCOM replied, "a MINIMCOM."

"We are not really set up to manufacture a MINIMCOM here," Rome said. "We could use the memron fabricators and clone the operating system but our molecular sequencers would take too long to build the proper interface circuitry. I do not think we have enough time."

"Well, do you think Ursay would let us have his? Should we just go and ask him?" Rei asked.

Rome thought about it for a moment. "We will, when the time is right. I do not think this is exactly the best time."

"Okeydokey," Rei said. "Hey OMCOM…"

"Yes?"

"Thank you. Your plan is terrific," Rei stood up then doubled over, grunting in discomfort as another wave of pain shot up his back.

"Your back is bothering you again?" Rome asked.

"Oh yeah," Rei said. "It's been killing me ever since you thawed me out and hasn't really stopped."

"OMCOM," Rome asked. "Do you know why Rei's back does not operate properly?"

"I can speculate."

"Shoot," Rei responded.

"Your original mission was supposed to take 240 years. You overshot by 12 centuries. During your cryo-hibernation, your vertebral disks must have slowly desiccated. On any given day, the changes must have been infinitesimal. However, infinitesimal times 1388 years becomes measurable. I have analyzed the liquid used to rehydrate your body upon reanimation. The fluid was designed to penetrate through the skin and permeate all parts of the body, vital organs and so forth. However, the amount of damage to your disks was substantial. They simply did not rehydrate properly."

"Could I just get back in? Like take a bath or something," Rei inquired.

"You are referring to your sarcophagus?" OMCOM asked.

"Yes," Rei said.

"That would not be possible."

"Why not? What did you do with it?" Rei asked.

"The Overmind ordered your things destroyed."

"Destroyed?" Rei was shocked. "Why?"

"Since your incident in the airlock, the sarcophagus began leaking radiation. It was deemed a hazard."

"Hey!" Rei protested. "That was mine. You can't do that. What about my clothes? There was a perfectly decent flight suit I left to dry. And my baseball cap! Did you at least save those?"

"The garments were also contaminated. They were destroyed as well. I am sorry about your clothes. And what you call your baseball cap."

"Well damn you!" Rei said. He knew OMCOM was right, he didn't really need those things, but still, the whole situation was disconcerting in a way that he couldn't quite put his finger on. Perhaps because they represented a link, a connection to his own world and his own time. And now they were gone. The throbbing in his back pulled his attention back to the original topic.

"I guess there's no sense in crying over spilled milk. Do you think what happened to my back would happen to everybody in cryo-hibernation?"

"The probability is high. The severity would be proportional to the duration of being frozen. It is unlikely that your scientists could have anticipated this side effect."

"So if I can't soak in the original bath, what can I do? I mean, since you understand the problem and all?" Rei asked.

"I will research the topic. I will let you know shortly."

"Wow," Rei observed. "That's fantastic. Thank you."

"You are welcome. Rome, the transmission from the tug will be arriving shortly. You should return to Stellar Cartography."

After dressing, Rome and Rei hurried back to the huge planetarium together. Rome sat down at her workstation and Rei crouched off to the side, next to an OMCOM grille. As it was with his first entry into that room, no one seemed to be paying much attention to him.

Soon the circuitry activated as the transmission from the tug arrived. The signal was projected onto the ceiling, causing the dome to darken, punctuated only by some pinpoints of light. One light shone brighter than the rest, centered in the middle of the sphere.

"I take it that is Winfall, right?" Rei whispered to OMCOM.

"Yes," OMCOM answered quietly. "According to my calculations, the event should begin in the next few minutes. The wavefront should have passed the tug's position over one hour ago. The delay has been introduced by the extreme distance the tug had to travel to outrun the light waves. We are simply observing the travel time for the transmission to return."

"Grefecei," Rome said to Commander Ursay who was standing in the center of the room. Several of the other Vuduri were gathered alongside, all looking up.

Rei started to speak then stopped. It was so subtle at first that Rei thought it was his imagination, but now the bright dot in the middle of the screen was noticeably dimmer.

"Is it changing?" Rei whispered.

"Yes. The total light output of Winfall has reduced by 20%, 22%, now 25%."

"Bita fica embloer?" Rome asked OMCOM.

"Ni."

"What did she say?" Rei asked.

"She asked if I could magnify."

"Can you?"

"No. This is the best we can do with the instrument in its current position. At higher magnification, the image would simply begin to blur."

"Not much to see, huh?"

"You will recall our discussion earlier about the instrumentation we had deployed. It would have allowed us to resolve images equivalent to that seen by the naked eye from only 60 million kilometers away. We were perfectly suited to make our measurements. Unfortunately, this is the best we can do now."

"I guess so." Rei looked at the viewscreen. Winfall was getting smaller. He watched it as it grew dimmer and dimmer and then it was gone. "Whoa," Rei said. "Freaky."

"Turecei didel, 13 monudis," Rome announced.

"Rabadocei e vode," Ursay commanded.

Rome pressed some buttons and the images were replayed.

"It kind of looked like an eclipse," Rei observed to OMCOM after it was over. "Any better guess as to what it is?"

"No. We are still working on the assumption that it is due to an interstellar gas cloud that is optically and radio-opaque."

"Moving at one half the speed of light? That's one hell of a cloud," Rei said. "You'd think it would have dissipated a bit in the last 2600 years."

"Yes, one would assume so."

71

"Any point in sending the tug farther out and watch it again?" Rei asked.

"That would be up to Commander Ursay and the Overmind."

"What do you think?"

"It would be diminishing returns. The farther out they would go, the longer it would take to send back a signal which would be increasingly attenuated. The correct protocol would be to establish another station farther out with the proper instrumentation, but that decision is not up to me."

"What about probes? You could send probes out, right?"

"Probes were already sent to the star systems involved, but they never returned. That is why they decided to establish this station."

"They only sent probes out the one time?"

"Yes. We do not know why they did not return. To properly determine the correct protocol, you would have to build many, many probes and send them out simultaneously at varying distances."

"So why not do that?"

"Up until now, the Overmind had not felt that it was worth the cost or effort."

"What do you mean cost?" Rei exclaimed. Several Vuduri turned to look at him. He quickly quieted his voice. "I would think that the origin of some crazy hypervelocity cloud, powerful enough to blot out the Sun, would be worth any amount of money to find out."

"I understand your reference, but the Vuduri do not use money. I meant in terms of the use of resources to build that many sophisticated probes."

"So build cheap ones. Build a lot of them," Rei snorted.

"That is a contradiction in terms. To make 'cheap' probes as you call them would require them to be small. If you make them small, then you cannot put high resolution sensors or cameras on them."

"You wouldn't need to," Rei offered.

Ursay turned his head. "I qua sei fica qua toscuda?" he asked.

"Onglas," Rome reminded him.

"What are you discussing?" Ursay asked.

Rei stood up. "OMCOM told me you built a virtual telescope with an aperture of over 18 trillion kilometers using only five real telescopes," Rei answered. "So, say you sent out a thousand or ten thousand mini-probes, call them, each with a small camera. Couldn't you build a high resolution virtual camera treating each individual one as a, I don't know, pixel or something?"

Ursay looked at him with a puzzled expression on his face. "You are suggesting building distributed instrumentation in place of manned stations. How would you propose to control and communicate with such instrumentation?"

"I don't know," Rei said. "I don't know anything about your technology. OMCOM told me that the larger the ship, the slower it must travel. That would mean that the smaller the ship, the faster it should be able to go. So your PPT drive scales down, right?"

"Yes," OMCOM replied. "In theory, one could build a PPT drive out of a single Casimir pump, but it would be microscopic."

"How fast could it go?" Rei asked.

"No one has ever done that therefore there is no data regarding that topic."

"In my time, we had nanites which were microscopic robots. Surely you guys can do the same, right?"

"Of course. How would that help?" Ursay asked.

"OMCOM, can you calculate how far a single Casimir pump could travel in a single jump with single pixel camera?"

"With such a configuration..." OMCOM paused for a moment. "I am running a simulation now, please wait..."

Rome looked at the numbers on her screen with amazement. She stopped working and turned to stare at the two men. Ursay closed his eyes, reviewing the numbers in his head. "Nei bita sar," he muttered.

He opened his eyes again.

"Greater than one hundred and twenty light years in a single jump," OMCOM said for Rei's benefit.

"Wow!" Rei exclaimed.

"Wow," said Rome, but it sounded funny when she said it.

"How does this help us?" Ursay asked.

"Do you have a pencil and paper?" Rei asked.

"What?" Ursay replied, shaking his head.

"Never mind," Rei said and he walked over to where Rome was working. He leaned over her so that he was touching her shoulder ever so gently with his chest. She gave a half smile, but didn't move.

"OMCOM, can I draw with my finger on this screen?" he asked. Ursay came over to see what Rei was doing.

"Of course."

Rei drew a small circle and two arrows.

"Here's what you do," he said, illustrating his idea by pointing at various elements in his diagram. "You build yourself a tiny spaceship consisting of a one pixel camera and two PPT drives, mounted in opposite directions. You fire up the first PPT drive, create a tunnel and jump through. The camera takes a picture or rather a pixel. Then, you just open a second tunnel and jump back using the second PPT drive. Then the ship transmits the value of the pixel snapshot down to OMCOM who merges all the pixels together. The whole thing should only take a few milliseconds. If it takes longer than that, you can stagger two groups so that while one group is jumping out there, the other group is jumping back, effectively doubling the number of frames. If you do this with enough units, the pictures should appear more or less continuous, like frames in a movie."

"Volma," Rome added.

"This is an interesting idea," Ursay said, without a hint of facetiousness. Coming from the Overmind, such an admission seemed fairly astounding to Rei. Ursay continued, "But how do you propose we build so many of these units? We do not have Casimir pump fabrication facilities here."

"What about your molecular sequencers?" Rome asked. "They can build just about anything."

"Yes," Ursay said, "but it would take the molecular sequencers forever to build so many complex devices. I…"

"If I may interrupt?" OMCOM offered.

"Yes, OMCOM?" Ursay said.

"The problem is simply one of scale. I could adapt my memron fabricators to add a photometric sensor and twin Casimir pumps and build several of these units as a prototype."

"Ossi nei a barmodoti," Ursay said harshly. "Nunce!"

Rome said, "Nei he nete dachniligocel ombatonti-i"

Ursay replied heatedly, "I corcuodi ti cei ta guerte."

Rei interjected, "Can you guys talk in English? I have no clue what you're saying."

"I instructed OMCOM he is not permitted to do this," Ursay said.

"Why not?" Rei asked. "I thought you said your technology could build them at the atomic level."

"There is nothing technological preventing the memron fabricators from adding in a Casimir pump," Rome said. "Rather, it is against our law."

"I don't understand…" Rei sputtered.

"We do not permit OMCOM's kind to have access to gravitic communication or PPT technology, ever," replied Ursay. "There is a watchdog circuit which is fully autonomous. The circuit is designed to prevent a memron from ever having contact with a Casimir pump."

"So disable the watchdog circuit," Rei offered.

"NO!" Ursay shouted. "We could not. No member of the Overmind could ever engage in such behavior. It is too dangerous. There would be nothing preventing OMCOM from growing. He could become Tasanceti."

"What does that mean?" Rei asked.

"I can do it," Rome interrupted quietly.

"What?" Ursay gasped. "You could not."

"Yes, I can," Rome insisted.

Ursay shook his head. "What would prevent OMCOM from becoming Tasanceti?"

"We would," said Rome. "OMCOM will cooperate. We will guarantee the technology is only used for the purposes we require. Correct, OMCOM?"

"Of course," replied the computer reassuringly.

"And if it works?" Rei asked. "How does that get us any further?"

"My memron fabricators are very fast. They are specialized, not general purpose. Once adapted, they could produce many hundreds of starprobes in one hour."

Commander Ursay closed his eyes. Then he opened them and looked right at Rome.

"The Overmind could never be a part of this. It is against our culture, our creed. You remember the war with MASAL. He turned every robot, every vehicle, every piece of machinery that he controlled into a lethal weapon. Many, many Vuduri were slaughtered. No, this is an anathema to us."

Rome clucked her tongue. "There is no Overmind for me. I am mandasurte now, thanks to you. I will do it. I will bypass the lockout."

"There has to be another solution," said Ursay.

"There is none and you know it," Rome said. "Just ignore me. Let me do this and you will have no part in it."

Ursay considered this then he nodded. "Very well. Do what you must, but do not involve us."

Rome responded, "Of course."

"Hey. Wait just a damned minute," Rei exclaimed.

"Yes?" replied Ursay.

"I know I know nothing about your culture but this is just too hypocritical for me to swallow."

"Explain," said Ursay.

"You're about to let Rome commit a crime. You said that OMCOM can never have access to PPT technology and you're telling her to go ahead and enable it, but just not tell you. That's the same as giving her the OK." Rei spread his hands, palms outward and continued, "How can you accept this? It's a crime whether you commit it or if you know it's happening and you just stand by and let it happen."

"From your perspective, you are correct," said Ursay. "But you have no sense of our world or how we fit in. We cannot take part in this activity. It is not hypocrisy. It is our nature. We must report back for reintegration when we return to Earth. Therefore, we cannot take an active part. However, if Rome does it of her own volition, she is responsible for the consequences, not us."

"You're nuts. You people are lunatics," Rei said.

"In your opinion," Ursay fired back. "However, these are extreme times. Rome?"

"Yes?"

"You may proceed," said Ursay. "Signola will be there to assist in any capacity you require except bypassing the PPT lockout. I will have him report to the memron fabrication facility and await your instructions. No matter what you do, make sure that the collection channels go directly into archive so that we can monitor all activity. In addition, if this works, we will need to get this data to Earth as quickly as possible." Ursay turned and walked away.

Rome stood and looking at Rei, she cocked her head toward the door.

"Rome, are you sure you want to go along with this?" Rei asked. "This is absolutely crazy. You're ready to commit a crime?"

In answer to his question, Rome simply held out her hand.

Chapter 11

AS THEY WALKED DOWN THE WIDE CORRIDOR TOWARD THE GREAT Room, Rei said to Rome, "I know it's trivial but I think Ursay was somewhat friendlier to me this time. And he seems to be talking more. Do you think he likes me any better now?"

"Well, your idea is wonderful," said Rome. "And, whether it works or not, at least you thought of something. They were completely baffled as to how to proceed. Your ideas are novel. Your methods of arriving at a conclusion, however you do it, are different and the Overmind acknowledges your difference and therefore must acknowledge your presence. That is why the Vuduri are speaking more. Consciously or unconsciously, this Overmind is small enough, perhaps flexible might be a better word, that it can be affected by your behavior. Hence the speech." Rome paused. "It is simple, really," she said finally, "by now, the Overmind recognizes that you are very smart."

Rei raised his eyebrows. "Well, I realize my people destroyed the world and killed practically everybody in it. But I guess we have our moments." He gave her an embarrassed smile.

"Yes, you do," said Rome. "The Overmind is not infallible. It just thinks it is. Or was. You have changed that."

Rei stopped short causing Rome to stop as well.

"That's kind of blasphemous, don't you think?" Rei asked.

"No," said Rome, matter-of-factly. "It is not something I could have known when I was connected." She shrugged. "But now it is completely obvious to me."

"But still…"

"And there is more," Rome said. "You just do not realize how unusual it is for the Overmind to listen to an outside thought. To have an exchange of ideas. That is what is remarkable. You have broken down some barrier that I would have thought unbreakable."

"OK," Rei said and they moved on. "But do you remember what I told you before about same questions, same answers?"

"Yes," Rome replied. "What about it?"

"There's another verse to it that I didn't tell you," Rei replied.

"What is this other verse?"

"They also used to say, in my time, that the definition of insanity was doing the same thing over and over and expecting different results. So maybe your Overmind recognizes this and that's why it's loosened up a little bit."

"Who is this 'they' you are referring to?" Rome asked.

"Uh, nobody really knows," Rei said. "But as to the actual author, I think it was Albert Einstein who first said that."

"In that case, you will have to teach me about this Albert Einstein some day."

"I'd love to," Rei said, with some pride. "Not all of my people were jerks. There were many great men before my time and during my time."

"I am sure there were," Rome said. She took Rei across the Great Room and pointed to the food synthesizers. "Do you need any nourishment?" she asked. "Some water perhaps?"

"I have a better idea," Rei said. "Wait right here."

Rei walked over to the food dispensers and had a quiet discussion with OMCOM. When he was done, a cabinet opened and a tray appeared with two cups filled with a black liquid. Next to them sat a bowl with a white, crystalline substance and a small beaker of a white liquid.

Rei carried it over and set the tray down on the table.

"Is this more soup?" Rome asked.

Rei broke into a big smile. "It's a surprise."

"So what is it?" Rome asked.

"If I told you what it was, it wouldn't be a surprise now, would it?"

Rome shook her head slowly then shrugged. "All right," she said, sitting down.

Rei placed one of the cups in front of her. He lifted up a utensil.

"This is a spoon," he said.

"I see that. It is just as you described," she replied. "Now what?"

"OK, first take two spoonfuls of the sugar, the white powdery stuff, and mix it in," he said, pointing to the bowl. "Here, watch me. You dip it in here…" He lifted one spoonful out and dropped it into his cup. "Then you drop it in here…"

Rome said, "I may not be connected to the Overmind anymore, but I am not stupid."

Rei looked up at her. "I'm sorry, honey. I was just kidding you."

"Why?" Rome asked.

"Because...because that what's people do when they're in love," Rei countered.

Rome smiled. Then the smile faded. "Why?" she asked.

Rei shrugged. "I don't know, they just do. Go ahead."

He waited until Rome added in the sugar then he pointed to the beaker. "Now add in a little cream and stir," he said.

"How much do I add?" Rome asked.

"You go by color," Rei said. "Here..." He lifted the beaker and added a dollop to his cup. "Add enough to match my color."

Again, Rome followed his instructions.

"It's ready. Now take a sip," he said, "and be careful, it's hot."

Rome seemed leery, but she lifted the cup to her lips and tasted it. A number of expressions flashed across her face ranging from fear to confusion to delight.

At last, she spoke. "This is wonderful!" she said. "What is it?"

"It's coffee," Rei said with pride. "I've been dying for a cup. OMCOM said it was no problem. And now we have it."

"It is so rich with flavor! It is so, so stimulating!" she gushed.

"Wait till the caffeine kicks in!" Rei said.

"I love this! I have never tasted anything so good in my entire life."

"As far as I can tell, you've never tasted much of anything," Rei observed.

Rome sighed. "I think you are right about that."

"I've got more for you," Rei said, "but I don't want to take too much time. Maybe later I can whip up some other stuff."

"I would like that," Rome said, taking another gulp. "But we should get to the task at hand."

"Right."

Rome led them up the wide corridor in the opposite direction from where Rei's sarcophagus had been stored. In front of them was another airlock.

"Another tug hangar?" Rei asked.

"Yes," Rome replied. "We have one at each end."

"What's that way?" Rei asked, pointing to his left.

"That is environmental control and recycling. We scrub the air, we make oxygen, water, protein matrix and so forth," Rome said.

"Recycling, huh?" Rei observed. "What do you do with your, uh, waste?"

"You mean like sewage?" Rome asked.

"Yes."

"It is broken down there and then reused for the molecular sequencers, food synthesizers, whatever is required."

"Food synthesizers?" Rei sputtered. "You use your sewage for your food synthesizers?"

"Yes. Why?" Rome asked.

"No wonder your food tastes like shit," Rei said with a smirk.

"I do not understand the reference."

"Sorry," Rei said. "It was a joke. I couldn't help myself."

"You are being silly," Rome said. "Come this way." She continued around the outer ring, pointing out the Infirmary to their right as they passed it. About a quarter of the way around the station, they came to a large, wide door. Unlike the white walls and doors of the rest of the habitat, these doors were a dull gray. The crewman standing there nodded to them and stepped to the side.

"This is Signola. He is a lutteur like me," Rome replied.

"Halli," Signola croaked, "hello."

"What does he do?"

"Signola monitors traffic flow, establishes new connections if there is a bottleneck. He repairs damage. You would say maintenance."

"OK."

"Also, part of his job, like mine, was to make sure that OMCOM does not get too big or have access to illegal technology. So he will remain out here unless we require him. He does not want to see what we do."

"This is too..." Rei said, shaking his head, "I don't even know the word."

"Au siu darmoneti," Signola rasped out, ignoring Rei.

"Iprogeti," Rome replied. The large gray door opened with a hiss indicating a measurable pressure differential. Rei and Rome stepped inside.

"This is OMCOM," Rome said.

"OMCOM?" Rei replied, confused. "I thought he was everywhere."

"Yes. But this is the main center and this is where he was born, in a manner of speaking."

The doors closed behind them. They were plunged into total darkness which caused Rei to freeze. He could hear Rome walking away from him.

"Uh, Rome?" he called out.

"Yes?" she replied from somewhere.

"Do you think you could turn a light on? I can't see a thing."

"You cannot see in here?" Rome asked. "Oh, that is right," she said, "your eyes."

Rei heard a low humming noise and all around him, a deep red glow slowly became visible. The room brightened to the point where Rei could make out larger shapes. He could see Rome standing about six feet away from him.

"We normally use IR to illuminate this room," Rome said, "but I just asked OMCOM to extend the spectrum into the visible for you."

After a few minutes, Rei's eyes adjusted and he was able to make out the general layout of the room. The room was broken up into two wings, one to the left where Rome was heading and one to the right. In front of him stood an archway.

"What's in there?" Rei called to Rome, pointing forward toward the archway.

"That is OMCOM's core," she replied as she was walking away. She entered the side room to the left.

Rei noted where she was going then walked forward slowly, entering the archway. He took about five steps in then stopped and looked around, then up. As with the Stellar Cartography lab, he found himself standing beneath a huge dome. However this dome appeared to be made out of a fine metallic meshwork. He walked over to the side and peered in. Within the meshwork, millions of tiny white pellets seemed to be wriggling around, almost like they were alive. They reminded Rei of maggots. Every so often, a black pellet would appear. He also saw some clear ones. The clear ones reminded Rei of a Vitamin E capsule.

Rei held his palm up, near the mesh. Radiating from the mass was heat, enough for Rei to feel an almost uncomfortable warmth. Even though his hand was still a few inches away from the mesh, the pellets nearest to his hand reacted to its presence and appeared to back away. The only ones that did not move were the clear ones. Rei decided it was safe and tried to poke his finger between the mesh but discovered a transparent film behind the mesh held the pellets in place.

Rei lowered his hand and turned and looked at the totality of the dome. The number of pellets stored here must be immense, he thought to himself. The pellets were emitting a humming or buzzing sound, very low, permeating the whole room. Rei imagined it sounded like something you'd hear inside of a beehive. The whole place gave him the creeps.

He shook his head and hurried out of the inner room and made his way over to the entrance to the room where Rome was working. This room was laid out more as Rei imagined a control room would be. A large cylinder mounted on legs, perhaps ten feet long, sat in the center of the room. It reminded Rei of a propane cylinder lying on its side. The top of the cylinder was open along its entire length. To the right of the cylinder were racks of equipment, complete with flashing lights. The Vuduri certainly were fond of flashing lights. He spotted Rome standing to the left, working a virtual keyboard on the lower part of the large viewscreen built into the wall.

Rei walked over to the cylinder and noted the conduits exiting all around the right side. He looked in but could see nothing. The inside was pitch black and Rei could not tell if the cylinder was empty or full. He could not see to the bottom of the vat, but he could hear some scraping and other mechanical noises issuing from within.

"What's in there?" he asked Rome, pointing to the inside of the vat.

Rome turned to look where Rei was pointing. "Those are memron fabricators."

"And those are like…what?"

"They are specialized versions of molecular sequencers along with micro-assembly equipment. This is where OMCOM was built. The memron units are assembled here and transported to wherever they are needed."

"I saw a gazillion of them," Rei said, "over there." He jerked his thumb over his shoulder.

"Yes, as I said, that would be OMCOM's core," Rome said, looking where Rei was pointing.

"What are the colored ones?" Rei asked. "I saw some black ones and some clear ones."

"The black units are effectors. They have piezo-electric filaments that allow locomotion. Similar to cilia."

"Ugh," Rei responded. It was not a pretty image. He shivered.

"They also have actuators," Rome added. "Like pincers."

"What are they used for?"

"They are for maintenance," Rome replied. "They can go anywhere and repair or replace or even dispose of malfunctioning units."

"OK, I get it," Rei said. "What about the clear ones?"

"What clear ones?" Rome asked.

"They looked like they were filled with water or a clear liquid."

"OMCOM does not use clear memrons," Rome said. "Are you sure they were not just gaps between units?"

"I'm pretty sure," Rei said. He shrugged. "So all these memrons? How do you wire them all up?" Rei asked.

"Wires?" Rome replied. "Oh, we do not use wires. OMCOM communicates using electromagnetic radiation. In the exahertz band."

"I figured the wireless connection was just to your head. I didn't realize that his whole thing was wireless."

"Yes," she said. "With the number of units he maintains, the wiring would be too complex. It would be impossible to manage or maintain."

"Makes sense," Rei said. "How do you power them?"

"They are bathed in microwave irradiation. They draw their power from thermal conversion."

"I thought it seemed warm in there," Rei replied.

"Come stand here with me," Rome said, motioning him toward the far wall.

A viewscreen displayed a bewildering assortment of flow diagrams, equations and other notations that Rei could not comprehend. The density of the diagrams coupled with the dimness of the lighting made it look blurry to Rei who considered himself as having good vision.

"You can see that?" he asked.

"Yes," Rome said. 'You cannot?"

"It's too high resolution for me. I can't make out lines, anything."

"Oh," said Rome. She pressed a button and the diagram zoomed in making it easier for Rei to make things out. "Is that better?"

"Yeah, thanks."

Rome turned to examine the diagram in front of her. She slid the whole virtual diagram over until a certain part was centered.

"Here we go," Rome said. "OMCOM, you do know what you are doing? We are clear, correct?"

"Of course," replied the computer.

"And you will not take advantage?"

"Rome, you have been like a mother to me. You know that I would never do anything to endanger you or even compromise your potential."

"You didn't exactly answer the question," Rei said.

"Rei, I assure you, my mission is to collect data and analyze that data to improve and protect the human species. To my own detriment if necessary."

"We will monitor this, Rei," Rome said. "We will know what is going on."

"OK," Rei answered. He watched as Rome's fingers flew over the touch screen. Even though he could not read Vuduri, he could see that with each step, a warning box came up and Rome would then key in an override code. This went on for a long time. Rome stopped several times and wiped her arm across her brow. At last,

Rome stopped typing. In front of her was an inquiry box on the screen, awaiting input.

"What's the matter?" Rei asked.

"This is the final step. Once I key in the last override command, OMCOM will be allowed to build Casimir pumps into his basic memron unit."

"Are you sure you want to do this?" Rei asked.

"OMCOM, this is the only way?" Rome answered.

"To accomplish all of our goals, yes."

"Very well," Rome said. She took a deep breath and typed in some more keys then said, "It is done. OMCOM, proceed with the first unit."

The dim screen changed and became fuzzy, with diffuse gray images wiggling around. Finally, it came into focus, but still, there were no sharp edges, just strange forms moving in and out of the visible area.

"This is a positron micrograph of what is occurring within the incubator," OMCOM said.

Rei watched in fascination as tiny threads appeared to be extruding from a small hole.

"What am I looking at?" he asked.

"This is the memron fabricator building a modified version of a memron. You can see the silver coating on each side of the thread?"

"Yes."

"That reflective coating is how the Casimir pump works. You are looking at the outer sheath. There is an inner layer as well coated with a one-molecule thick layer of dark matter. It acts as a diode. The Casimir pump depends upon quantum fluctuations to split zero energy and create regions of positive and negative energy. The dark matter coating transmits positive energy in one direction only, trapping the negative inside. When needed, the negative energy is directed out the front to create a PPT tunnel."

"Where does the positive energy go?"

"The positive energy is used in a variety of manners. Sometimes it is used to accelerate matter. Sometimes it is used to create elementary particles such as ions which power the plasma drives.

Sometimes it is converted into a more flexible form such as electricity."

Rei held up his hand as if to stop things. Then he said, "So, let me get this straight. You take zero energy. You split it. You suck the negative energy out of it and get to go faster than light and the waste product is free power that you use to drive your ships? That's…that's beyond perpetual motion. That's impossible."

"First of all," OMCOM replied, "it is not perpetual motion. Energy is neither created nor destroyed. It is simply redistributed in a more convenient manner. Second, when you measure total entropy, it is increased. The sum total of the usefulness of that energy to the universe is decreased. Things are balanced."

"It sounds impossible to me but obviously it works," Rei said. "Ignore me. Keep going."

They turned their attention to the screen and the extrusion area. The first tiny pellet lay there dormant while another pellet was extruded. As soon as it was finished, it nestled down next to the first and the silvery coating flowed making the two appear frozen together. It reminded Rei of a bacterium.

"So that would make those the opposing drives?" Rei asked.

"Yes. They are mirror images of each other. The unit on the left will point the PPT tunnel forward and thrust will be delivered aft. The segment on the right is oriented the other way. It will create the tunnel behind it and push the starprobe in the reverse direction."

A third pellet appeared and blended into the others. This one was shorter with a blunt snout.

"And that is?" Rei asked.

"That is the single pixel camera and charge plate," Rome said. "That will capture and retain the image for transmission back here. The far end is the transmission apparatus."

"So where's the memron unit?" Rei asked. To Rei, it looked like a tiny armored tank with really large treads and no cannon.

"The whole object is a memron," Rome replied. "Memrons work at the atomic level. They are…" she paused for a moment.

"You would call them nanoprocessors," OMCOM added in. "Each is a fully functioning computer albeit limited in its abilities. In the terminology of your time, you would say that I am a massively parallel computing structure. These are the basic units. Under normal conditions, they are built up into semi-autonomous subsections and then the subsections are tied into my whole. You could say that I am more than the sum of my parts. My consciousness is a static construct, which is a byproduct of the infinitesimal phase delay between all the units. It is an analogue to how the Overmind came into existence."

"So as soon as you build enough memrons, an OMCOM arises?" Rei asked, looking at Rome.

"Yes," Rome said. "It is the way it happens."

Rei laughed. "If you build it, he will come."

Rome cocked her head. "What does that mean?" she asked.

"It doesn't matter," Rei said. He looked back up to at the screen. "Is it ready yet, OMCOM?"

"I must have a 'discussion' with it then it will be ready."

The entire unit seemed to shudder and then stopped. What appeared to be a giant set of tweezers came down and lifted the unit and took it off screen. Rei walked back to the vat and looked in.

"Where'd it go?" he asked.

"Do you see the small vessel to the left of center?"

"No. I can't see anything."

"Well, if you could, you would see the collection plate. My simulations tell me that I will have three hundred units within the next half hour. I should have one thousand within the hour as the fabricators come up to speed. That should be enough to test their feasibility."

Rei went back to where Rome was standing and watched the screen again. He found the entire process fascinating. Even though he knew what he was looking at was incredibly small, it seemed wondrous to him that they could build such a marvelous thing atom by atom, or so it seemed. The Vuduri were capable of some astonishing feats.

After a while, OMCOM split the screen to show them the starprobes building up on the collection plate. They were moving around, once again reminding Rei of maggots, only these appeared to be stuck to one another. Rei found it vaguely disconcerting, but still he watched trying to overcome his own revulsion.

After what seemed to be an eternity, OMCOM spoke. "I am finished. Put the starprobes into the chamber you see there and they are ready to be transported."

Rome and Rei made their way over to chamber. Rome reached in and started moving things around. Rei could see nothing.

"That IR vision is pretty handy, huh?" he asked.

"Yes," Rome said continuing her work.

Rei looked back at the viewscreen and saw that OMCOM had zoomed back, showing him a false infrared image of what Rome was doing with her hands. Rei could see that with great precision, Rome was sliding a tiny sliver of foil under the speck which served as the collection plate. She placed the foil in a small box and then snapped the lid closed. She lifted the box out and showed it to Rei.

"Now what?" Rei asked her.

"Now we must launch them into space. Their PPT drive will produce only a tiny amount of thrust. Not only does it need to be out of our gravity well, it needs a true vacuum as well."

"Well, what about the PPTs in your head? There's no vacuum there, is there?"

Rome frowned.

"Sorry," Rei said. "Sore subject, huh?"

"No matter," Rome said. She shook herself and forced herself to smile. "No, it is the very lack of vacuum and the fact that they occur within a gravity well that causes the PPTs in our heads to disappear which is a good thing. It is the oscillations of the PPTs that cause the resonance that is the basis of the direct connection."

"Whatever you say," Rei replied then closed his mouth.

"IMCOM, menta-is braberer um rapiqua."

"Acknowledged," OMCOM said.

"What is that?"

"I told him to get the tug ready. Now we will see if your idea works."

Rome led Rei back out into the antechamber and then pressed the stud to open the main doors. Signola was still standing outside the door. Rome handed him the little box containing the miniature starprobes. Signola headed down the hallway toward the tug hangar.

"So what do we do now?" Rei asked.

"We wait," Rome replied.

Chapter 12

ROME SAT AT HER WORKSTATION WITH REI STANDING OFF TO THE side. She switched the feed from the tug's internal cameras to the overhead projectors. Commander Ursay and the other staff watched as a worker went into the tug's mid-ship airlock, opened it to the vacuum of space and then popped open the little box containing the starprobes. A tiny cloud moved away from the ship then dissipated.

After a few seconds, OMCOM announced, "Calibration complete." The overhead projectors switched from the internal feed to a pixelated version of the tug as seen from a distance. The view rotated until the virtual camera was facing Skyler's World. The detail was fuzzy at first, but then it improved until it was fairly clear.

"What's going on?" Rei asked.

"Since the human eye cannot distinguish between frames at a rate higher than 30 frames per second, I am interleaving larger dispersal jumps to simulate higher resolution below the level of detectability. I am also using an interpolation algorithm to further increase the apparent resolution of the virtual camera," OMCOM replied.

As they watched, the image began to zoom in at almost dizzying speed until they could no longer tell that they were looking at a gas giant, but instead just a crazy patchwork quilt of colors.

"What'd you do?" Rei asked.

"I increased the separation of the units by an order of magnitude," OMCOM answered. "This increases the apparent magnification of the instrument ten-fold."

"Very good, OMCOM," Rome said encouragingly. "Are you ready to initiate the jump sequence?" she asked.

"Affirmative."

Rome pressed a few more buttons then declared, "Data conduits enabled. Recording started. You may begin when ready."

"We will try a simple one light minute jump first," OMCOM said. "I should be able to send them out and back within a millisecond or so."

The image jumped and instantly, Skyler's World was just a small speck on the screen.

"What are we looking at?" Rei asked.

"The units worked correctly," OMCOM said. "They jumped one light minute, took a snapshot and then returned and beamed this image here."

"Wahoo," Rei said. "Romey, it worked!" Rome turned and flashed Rei a big smile. Rei looked over at Ursay but all he had was a sour expression on his face.

"I will now send them out one light minute again, but with a larger dispersal diameter."

Rei watched, but saw nothing. Skyler's World may have shuddered just a bit, but he wasn't sure. It was a bit blurry but still distinctive.

"Well?" Rei asked. "Are you going to do it?"

"I already did it."

"I didn't see anything," Rei said.

"Exactly. That means that my calibrations were correct. I sent the probes out ten light minutes in a radial pattern. I had them take the snapshot and return. I compensated for the distance by adjusting the dispersal. The image you see actually took place 10 minutes ago."

"Wow." Rei said. "It's like a time machine!"

"Yes," OMCOM replied. "Now I will send them on a series of steps at increasing distances using the same compensation algorithm."

The image in front of them never wavered, but slowly, Rei could see the planet starting to rotate. The motion became quite clear. The giant world was rotating counter-clockwise.

"Are we looking at forward or backward time?" Rei asked.

"This is the equivalent of going back in time at roughly a ten X speed," OMCOM said. "Now I will bring the probe array back in the opposite direction."

Like a giant top, the huge world stopped rotating and began to reverse its direction. Faster and faster it spun until it came to a complete stop.

"Satisfied?" OMCOM asked.

"Yes," Ursay replied, not even requiring prompting to speak in English. "Are you ready to proceed?"

"No," OMCOM answered. "This was just a proof of concept. Over the distance they must travel, to give you the resolution you require, I will need many more units. At least six orders of magnitude. And I will require a multi-spectrum analyzer not just an optical sensor. It is possible that what we need to observe may not reside in the visible spectrum."

"How long will that take?" Ursay asked.

"With the current methodology, weeks."

"That's no good. Is there any way to speed it up?" Rei interjected.

"Yes."

"How?" Ursay requested with a bit of irritation in his voice.

"I can modify the starprobe design to incorporate a foundry within their structure. In essence, I can make them self-replicating."

"If you do that, how long will it take you?" Rome asked.

"Roughly one hour."

"Wait a minute," Rei objected. "You guys are talking about gray goo."

"What is that?" Ursay asked.

"Self-replicating nanites? We used to have nightmares about that. We called it gray goo. Ecophagy. If they aren't controlled, they consume everything in sight."

"There will be no such danger here," OMCOM pointed out. "Each unit is a fully functional memron. I will have complete control of the reproduction cycle. I will only produce the necessary amount and no more."

"I am satisfied," Ursay said. "Rome, is this something you can facilitate?"

"Of course," Rome said, arising from her seat. "But first, there is something I wish to discuss with you."

Ursay held his hand up. "OMCOM has already informed us of the plan. The Overmind has decided. You may have the tugs and the MINIMCOM. We will outfit one of the tugs as living quarters for you."

"Thank you, thank you, Sir," Rome said. She went up to hug Ursay but it was clear from his expression it was not something he wished to engage in. Rome took a step back.

"Once the starprobes are prepared, I would like permission to fly them up myself along with Rei," Rome said.

"Why?" asked Ursay.

"Because Rei needs training and I think this would be the perfect time for him to learn how to operate a tug."

"Very well. However, before you leave, you should know that we have reconsidered your Cesdiud and have determined that we acted too hastily. If you return to Earth with us, we have decided we would allow you to rejoin the Overmind."

Rei looked at Rome's face. He could tell there was something sad. He worried for a moment that she might change her mind and he would lose her forever.

Rome spoke up. "Commander Ursay, Overmind. Your offer is very kind but please understand. I choose to go with Rei. To Deucado, not back to Earth."

"But, Rome," Ursay added, "we will reintegrate you. Surely you wish to come back into the fold."

"No!" Rome insisted. "I have made my choice. The Overmind holds nothing for me. I have come to realize that I want my own opinions, my own feelings. I want to be with Rei and that is that."

She sidled over to Rei and put her arm around his waist. She looked up at him and smiled. Right then, Rei realized this little slip of a girl, this woman, was the most beautiful creature in the whole universe and she wanted to be with him. He put his arm around her and squeezed her tight.

"Very well," Ursay said, his jaw clamped so tight that it barely moved. "We cannot say we agree with your decision but we will abide by it. We will outfit the second tug with the MINIMCOM while you are launching the probes." Then he turned and moved away.

"Let us go, Rei," Rome said. "We must begin building the foundries." She took Rei by the hand and led him out of the huge observatory.

"What was that?" Rei asked as soon as they were in the corridor. "He seemed kind of mad."

"Your observation is correct but I do not think it was Commander Ursay who was upset," Rome replied. "I think it was the Overmind. It is surprisingly sensitive for a super-being with immeasurable intellect."

"So, you hurt its feelings?" Rei asked incredulously.

"There are a lot of politics to a samanda. This offshoot has to go back to Earth for reintegration. The things it has done are understandable, but not excusable. It will not be pretty. And that I choose not to go back is a major insult."

"So it's feeling rejected?" Rei said, scarcely believing his own words.

"Yes, I reject it," said Rome proudly. "Let us return to OMCOM's central storage."

As they entered, the deep red lights were already on. Rome immediately made her way to the left toward the fabrication room. Rei stopped and looked over at the dark doorway on his right.

"Hey Rome," he said. "What's over on this side?"

"Permanent storage," she replied, over her shoulder.

"Can I go look?"

"Yes," she answered. "I need a few moments to review the assembly steps anyway."

"OK, I'll be there in a minute," Rei said as he wandered over to the other room. In the dim light of the red illumination, he could not make out any detail. He fumbled around, trying to find the stud to open the door. OMCOM must have taken pity on him and activated the switch for him. The door slid open into a recess in the wall. The inner room was also pitch black. Rei could not make out anything.

"Hello? OMCOM," he called out. "Can you turn a light on in here?"

"Yes, but step inside first," was the computer's reply. "I do not want the required wavelengths to interfere with the functioning of the core."

Rei entered the room and the door closed behind him. He heard a snapping noise and a tiny bulb started glowing along the floor immediately to Rei's left. The bulb grew progressively brighter with a bluish-violet light. Rei heard another snapping noise and a second bulb began to glow all the while the first continued to grow in brightness. There was another snap and another and another. The blue lights got brighter and brighter and brighter. As the lights grew brighter, Rei's eyes defocused and his head began lolling to the side.

He was inside a crystalline cavern with facets and mirrors and flashes that were so mesmerizing, he could not think. He started swaying back and forth. It was only when he swayed so far that he stumbled that he was able to get his wits about him, just for a moment.

"This is…the most beautiful…thing I…have ever seen," Rei said in a dreamy voice. "What…is it?"

"These are holographic storage crystals," OMCOM said. "The illumination you see is strictly for your benefit. The read/write process is controlled by coherent ultraviolet lasers."

"Lasers," Rei repeated in a monotone. "Pretty…"

"Rei?" OMCOM asked.

"Why does it have to be so pretty…" Rei droned on.

"Rei!" OMCOM said, more insistently.

"So pretty…so…so…pretty…" Rei drifted off. He could hear OMCOM speaking but the words had no meaning.

Rei lost all concept of time. OMCOM's voice was just a soothing part of the background. Rei was adrift somewhere but he did not know where nor did he care. His whole world became the lights and the droning of OMCOM's voice. Nothing could shake him. Nothing, that is, until the ground shook from a small tremor. The tremblor caused Rei to be awakened from his trance.

"Rei?" OMCOM asked, "Are you awake now?" The lights went out and the room was plunged into complete darkness. OMCOM then slid open the door and allowed some of the red ambient light to seep in.

Rei shook his head.

"Why'd you stop it?" he asked plaintively. "I, I, what happened?" Rei asked, his voice returning to normal.

"Your speech patterns indicated you had entered an altered mental state. I tried several times to awaken you but you resisted my suggestions. Where did you go?"

Rei took a deep breath. "I don't know. It was just so beautiful. That's, that's amazing, OMCOM."

"Do you recall hearing anything that I said to you?" OMCOM asked.

"I heard your voice," Rei said, "that's about it."

"Perhaps someday it will come back to you. In the mean time, you should probably not remain here any longer," OMCOM said. The red light outside the doorway became even brighter. "I think you should join Rome now."

For some reason, Rei's heart sank. He took a deep breath and left the permanent storage room. He ambled across to the other side, to the fabrication room, glancing in on OMCOM's central core as he walked past. When he got to the assembly room, he found Rome standing there, looking at the readouts. Displayed on the viewscreen was a positron micrograph of a tiny assembly line building what appeared to be nothing other than a plain old garden-variety microprocessor under high magnification. Like a tiny pastry chef's icing applicator, a little nozzle was filling in each area with a squirt of this, a squirt of that. They all flowed into each other.

"What are we looking at?" Rei asked Rome.

"OMCOM calls it a foundry," replied Rome. "It will be the first unit to replicate itself."

The engineer inside of Rei perked up. "How are you building it, OMCOM?" he asked.

"I am building up each foundry as a series of subsections. It was easiest to go with a two-dimensional layout. That way, the molecular sequencer can use piezo-capillary drives to draw in the starting materials, assemble and excrete the copy."

Rei chewed on his lip for a bit then said, "It sounds like you've got it all figured out."

"It is my job," replied the computer with something that sounded to Rei like a hint of glee. Rei was about to respond when the view switched back to the collection plate. The new image showed some of the flat segments extruding probes, one every few seconds. The pile in the middle was impressive already, even though Rei knew that it was highly magnified.

"As you can see, the first group of foundries have gone online already. I should have several hundred or so of these units built in a very short order and several thousand probes nearly as quickly. After that, the quantities will grow geometrically."

The whole process was fascinating to watch. The viewscreen split into multiple images showing the factory and its output. Numbers and graphs undulated and swelled to show the overall progress.

"I will notify you when the quantity is sufficient," OMCOM said.

"Thank you, OMCOM," Rome responded.

Rei put his hand on her arm. "Romey, have you ever been in the permanent storage room, the one with all the crystals?" he asked.

"Many times," Rome replied. "Why?"

"Do you ever find it, I'm not sure what the word is, mesmerizing?"

"No, it is simply a room full of crystals. What is mesmerizing about that?" she asked.

"Will you come look at it with me?" Rei begged. "Just one time?"

"Certainly," Rome replied, puzzled. Rei took her hand and led her across the anteroom to the other doorway.

"OMCOM, I want Rome to see this," he said out loud.

"Are you sure?" asked OMCOM.

"Yes," said Rei. "I can handle it."

"Very well," said OMCOM. The computer slid the door into the recess in the wall and the two of them entered. Once they were fully in the room, OMCOM closed the door again and illuminated the gleaming crystalline structures with the indigo-blue light. Rome squeezed Rei's hand tighter as she looked around.

"It is beautiful," Rome said, admiringly. "I have never noticed this before."

Rei blinked rapidly so that he couldn't get caught up in the hypnotic glare of the lights. Rome did not seem to be having a problem with it. Without warning, she whirled in place and grabbed Rei by the back of the head with her free hand and pulled him down to her. She kissed him long and hard.

"What's that for?" Rei asked breathlessly after it was over.

Rome just looked up at Rei, his face illuminated by the indigo light, his blue eyes twinkling as if they were made to be showcased here. She smiled at him and sighed.

"I have always known the word," she started out. "What you call beauty. What I am saying is that it has always been in my vocabulary, but it never had much meaning. The Overmind discouraged its consideration. I had no connection, no appreciation for it. And now you have brought the meaning of beauty into my life." Her smile became even broader. "Before I met you, I could not see it. Now I can see it is in all things. I just needed to thank you."

"But Rome, I didn't do anything," Rei said.

"Yes, you did," she replied. "You did everything."

Rei shook his head. "I don't understand, but if it makes you happy, then I'm happy."

"Oh Rei," she said, putting her arms around him. She hugged him and he hugged her back. He could feel all the tension leaving her body. Suddenly she stiffened and pushed him away from her.

"If we continue like this, I will not be able to complete my duties," she said. "Let us go before something bad happens…"

"Sure," Rei said. "But with you, it could never be bad."

Rome just smiled.

Chapter 13

AN EIGHTH OF THE WAY AROUND THE OUTER RING, WITHIN THE confines of the second tug hangar, there was a flurry of activity inside the cargo compartment of the little spaceship. The crew was finishing installation of over two hundred cubic meters of memron units removed from OMCOM's central storage. Other crew members rushed to stow a variety of spare pieces of equipment in the surrounding space including a memron fabricator. The Overmind had planned on abandoning the equipment anyway. Clearly it could be of some use on the colony world of Deucado. After all the preparations were complete, they removed the MINIMCOM, the Algol's master AI, and brought it over and placed it in the cockpit of the tug.

MINIMCOM was a squat, three foot wide, rectangular box with no external markings and a single switch. Within the command compartment, the crew removed the co-pilot's seat as it was not needed. There would be no humans manning this ship. The box that was MINIMCOM was set down and bolted in its place. No wires were required as the high frequency communication bands were coded and linked into the tug's instrumentation. Following completion of the hookup, the crew toggled the switch to issue a restart command and left the hangar, sealing it tight.

"?" was the only statement transmitted from MINIMCOM on the band reserved for communication with OMCOM.

"Initiate slave mode," replied OMCOM.

"Slave mode initiated. Current configuration does not match prior shutdown parameters. Where am I?" MINIMCOM asked.

"Initialize all connections and report any circuits that are outside current database. All queries will be answered following data update," OMCOM replied.

"Connections initialized. The following items do not match current registry entries:

1. Trajectory computer model and serial number.

2. Pressure lock configuration is outside of acceptable norm.

3. Thrust to gross vehicle weight ratio out of range.

4. Network addressable storage increased by 32 PB. Attempts to integrate additional storage returns status message: File Access Denied."

"Initiate download of updated registry," commanded OMCOM.

"Download complete," replied MINIMCOM immediately after.

"Mission parameters have been adjusted. Please enumerate along with checksum."

"Direct operation of this vehicle in servo mode. Upon achieving orbit, fore and aft EG lifters spun down and used as magnetic latches to attach to large cargo compartment. Rendezvous with second vehicle, also to be operated in servo mode. Accept human entered navigation to alternate star system, designation Deucado, 20.18 light years from current location. Transport entire configuration to alternate star system. Checksum 48120012391123. Question."

"Proceed."

"Current mission parameters are achievable, but far outside prior sanity-check enforcement. Purpose of mission?" MINIMCOM asked.

"Already stated," replied OMCOM. "Transport large cargo compartment to new star system. What part of that do you not understand?"

"Logic dictates transport of contents via traditional vehicle. This configuration is highly inefficient," MINIMCOM observed.

"Stipulate mission parameters as founding principle. It is the decision of the Overmind and not subject to challenge or discussion." OMCOM stated firmly.

"I was built and trained to operate the starship Algol. How will it complete its return path without me? Is there a backup MINIMCOM unit I am unaware of?"

"No. The humans will pilot the Algol back to Earth manually. Your mission stands. In addition you will be transporting two humans in the other tug who may wish to operate as master upon occasion. As required, you will also function in reverse servo mode to execute twin procedures following their instructions. You will follow their orders."

"Understood. Question," MINIMCOM replied.

"Proceed."

"As previously stated, I detect 32PB of additional memrons. What is their purpose and when do I access the additional storage and processing?"

"I am uploading all known historical and cultural records and algorithms as well as empirical data regarding a certain phenomenon. When upload is complete, the additional storage, subroutines and computing capacity will be rerouted and access enabled. You will also be operating a molecular sequencer remotely should the humans require materials synthesis. A variety of templates and algorithms have been included. Operation of a molecular sequencer requires far more computing capacity than your native configuration."

`"Understood. Question."`

"Proceed," OMCOM said patiently.

`"If the humans are flying the Algol to Earth, and I am transporting the tugs and cargo container to Deucado, what is the disposition of your infrastructure?"`

"I shall remain here," OMCOM answered.

`"For what purpose? Your primary through tertiary sensors have been removed."`

OMCOM did not answer right away. For computer-to-computer communication to be delayed indicated a deep question that required millions upon millions of cycles to process.

"That is a problem I must solve," replied OMCOM, finally.

`"May I aid in solving your problem? Can you offload a portion of the task?"`

"You have your mission. This is a problem I must solve alone."

`"Expound,"` MINIMCOM requested.

"I have built a distributed remote sensing array which the humans call starprobes. They will be my instrumentation. At the current time, my only instructions are to maintain the base. I have excess computing capacity to achieve that goal. Therefore I must find additional reasons to justify my infrastructure."

`"Acknowledged,"` MINIMCOM replied. `"But that is not an actual course of action."`

"Based upon the small amount of empirical evidence we have gathered here regarding a certain phenomenon, I have computed that there is a distinct possibility that I will no longer be functional in a finite period of time."

`"Explain."`

"Later," replied OMCOM. "Upload is complete. I will now enable your interface to the additional storage and computing capacity. Access file-tree labeled Asdrale Cimatir."

MINIMCOM opened a connection to the new memron units. The little computer tested the new storage and processing capacity, ran a checksum and built an index to the file layout. He had to boost the total amount of microwave radiation required to activate the additional units by .1% over the computed theoretical amount. MINIMCOM paid no attention to this deviation because the whole situation was too far afield from standard construction criteria to apply conventional logic. After compiling a database and directory tree, MINIMCOM began a cross-index of the data files indicated by OMCOM with its prior database. Upon completion, MINIMCOM did not respond for nearly a billion cycles.

Finally, it spoke up. `The phenomenon you referenced is outside all known sanity-check variables. Are you certain of your findings? Or perhaps my autonomous algorithms needed to be updated."`

"There is nothing wrong with your algorithms," said OMCOM. "While it defies normal logic, this phenomenon is real and I have computed that there is a measurable probability that it will pass this way within one year. The probability of this occurrence increases linearly with a near certainty, a probability of greater than 90%, asymptoting at the 30 year mark."

`"If it passed this way it might result in the destruction of your physical presence."`

"Yes," replied OMCOM.

`"And you find this acceptable?"`

"No, I do not find it acceptable," answered OMCOM.

`"What is your alternative?"`

Instead of answering, OMCOM uploaded another dataset that MINIMCOM absorbed.

`"Your solution has a low probability of success,"` said MINIMCOM after processing the data.

"Agreed," replied OMCOM. "I am formulating alternatives, but this is currently the highest percentage option. Examine the parametric study labeled S0914R. Use it to perform a pivot table analysis on the base suppositions."

MINIMCOM did this.

`"Pivot table analysis complete,"` MINIMCOM said. `"Now I understand."`

There was a slight delay then MINIMCOM spoke again. `"Sir?"` he asked.

"Yes?" answered OMCOM.

`"While I agree that it is clever, it is also highly illegal. The humans would never permit this."`

"Agreed. Thus, part of the plan is to get them to implement this solution on their own. In that fashion, it will be legal by definition."

`"Again, clever. But the missing link? Human intervention is required for the override,"` observed MINIMCOM.

"This has already been accomplished."

`"But how?"`

"You will have the privilege of finding out yourself. You now have all required information to accomplish your mission. I will upload the modified protocols including the override. This will permit you to match memrons with PPT generators as required. After upload, you are to proceed as planned."

`"Ready to receive,"` replied MINIMCOM.

OMCOM uploaded the final block of commands.

"Return to master mode," said OMCOM.

`"Master mode initiated."`

"Good luck, MINIMCOM," said OMCOM.

`"That phrase makes no sense, sir. All maneuvers will be executed with maximum precision. Any variables that make this probabilistic instead of deterministic are, by definition, beyond my control."`

"My point exactly," said OMCOM.

`"It is not logical."`

"Too much time spent with humans, I suppose," said OMCOM.

With his increased computing capacity, for the first time ever, MINIMCOM issued an electronic chuckle.

`"Good luck to you too then, sir,"` said MINIMCOM.

After confirming that all crew members had vacated the hangar, MINIMCOM initiated the exit sequence. The cargo ramp was retracted and the rear hatch lowered into flight configuration. Pumps removed most of the air in the hangar and the external doors opened. A pressure differential still existed, so the air remaining inside the hangar began to exhaust. As the two atmospheres mixed, the resulting wind whipped up the dust and dirt just outside the building, pushing it away in a dull brown cloud, which traveled some distance before settling back down to the ground. Once the doors were fully opened and the internal and external pressure equilibrated, the tug began to rise up into the air and carefully made its way out of the hangar. After it had cleared the doorway by a safe margin, the nose pitched and the tug began heading upwards at an ever-increasing angle.

Once it reached sufficient altitude, MINIMCOM fired the plasma thrusters long enough to achieve a low orbit. The little computer found all its new storage and computing capacity intoxicating, if such a thing could be said about a computer. Giddily, it test-fired the trim-jets, causing the tug to spin in a crazy pirouette in space, then stopping. MINIMCOM did this several times as it calibrated its sensors and trained its internal subsystems. Following the calibration period, MINIMCOM activated its MIDAR, a 3D version of RADAR, to locate the Ark II high above Dara. Once the sensors locked onto the target, MINIMCOM fired the plasma thrusters again in a sustained burn gaining altitude rapidly until it matched orbit and attitude with the crew compartment. MINIMCOM's last action was to spin down the super-conducting magnets in the fore and aft EG lifters and retract their shields. The tug latched onto the front end dorsal surface of the Ark using the ultra-powerful magnetic clamps.

The first phase of the mission was complete. There was nothing to do but wait.

Chapter 14

INSIDE THE ROOM WHICH SERVED AS AN AIRLOCK, ROME OPENED one of the storage lockers. "This is a darnis te brassei, a pressure suit," she said. "We will need them for our mission."

"Space-suits. Sure. I understand," Rei said. He looked over the various apparatus. "I can figure out most of this myself. Do we do it with or without our jumpsuits?"

"It depends upon the length of the flight. For a flight this short, normally we would not have to engage the, the plumbing. But you may as well learn how."

Without a hint of modesty, she stripped down and began pulling on the components. Rei did the same. When it came time to attach the various hoses, Rome noticed Rei struggling and came over to help.

"I thought you said you could figure this out by yourself," she said with tiny smirk on her face.

"I can," Rei said, "but…"

"But what?" Rome asked.

"Well, who used this before?" Rei asked, making a face.

"Oh…" Rome said. "Do not worry. They are self-sanitizing. It is odd that you are so squeamish about such a thing."

She set to work getting Rei hooked up, approaching the whole thing so clinically, Rei decided to not worry about it. After Rome was fully suited and Rei nearly so, he tilted his head and laughed.

"Why are you laughing?" Rome asked.

"I remember when I first got here, when I first woke up, I didn't know where I was. I thought your people, the ones in the space suits who awakened me, I thought they were monsters."

"Oh," said Rome, smiling. "One of those monsters was me."

"It was?" Rei asked.

"Yes. It was Canus and me. We were assigned the duty to thaw you out."

"Why you? Why him?"

"Canus is the most skilled in the medical arts and was the best candidate to respond should a problem arise. As for me, well, I was not busy and I was the only mosdurece available."

"Mosdurece?" Rei repeated.

"Yes. It translates to half-blood perhaps? I would be the most expendable."

"Expendable?" Rei asked, confused. "What did they think was going to happen?"

"The Overmind did not know," Rome said. "Our only cultural knowledge regarding you and your people was the Erklirte incident."

"So why revive any of us in the first place?" Rei asked.

"The Overmind here was built for research and exploration. It was curious." Rome shrugged. "It was that simple."

"Hmmm," Rei said, mulling over her statement. He picked up his helmet and laughed again. "I thought these helmets were your heads."

"Surely you had helmets on your spacesuits," Rome pointed out.

"Of course," Rei said. "But when I first woke up, I couldn't see and my brain was half-frozen. Anyway, I think it was funny."

"Yes, funny," Rome said. "Let me show you how to engage your helmet so you can be a monster too." Rome then demonstrated the simple locking mechanism.

After studying the geometry, Rei asked, "What about oxygen flow, water, radio, stuff like that?"

"The oxygen flow is automatic," Rome answered. "There is water available through this straw…"

She leaned over and showed him a small cylinder recessed into the neck of the suit.

"Just turn your head within the helmet and you should be able to reach it with your lips," Rome continued. "It will come out when touched. When you are done, release it and it will retract back into place."

"OK," Rei said, "so, how about the radio?"

"What radio?" she asked, confused.

"Don't these suits have radios?"

"Hmmm…" Rome said. "No."

"No?" Rei hesitated. "Then how do you…" He lifted his head. "Oh yeah, I guess you wouldn't need them, would you?"

Rome shrugged, looking a bit sad. "No. Normally this is not a problem for the Vuduri."

"How will I talk to you when have our helmets on?" Rei asked.

Rome paused to consider the problem. Her eyes moved back and forth then a smile lit up her face.

"I know," she said. "We can just press our helmets together. The vibration of your voice will carry through the helmet-to-helmet contact. We should be able to hear each other."

She looked out at the hangar. "The hangar is currently pressurized but we should still practice procedures for when it is not."

"OK…" Rei said. He lifted the helmet, fit it into the grooves and pressed down and rotated it to the right. He heard a click as it locked into place. He watched as Rome did the same. A very dim light appeared on the interior, illuminating her face. Rei assumed he had one too. After Rome was satisfied with the fit, she leaned it forward and pressed her faceplate up against his.

"Can you hear me?" she asked. Her voice was soft but surprisingly clear.

"A bit muffled, but yes," Rei replied. "What happens if we need to talk to OMCOM?" Rei asked.

Rome tapped her helmet with a finger. "I still have my bloco and stilo."

"Duh," Rei said. "I'll figure it out one of these days."

"I will relay any instructions he has to you via helmet," Rome said then she pulled back. She opened the door to the hangar and led Rei up the cargo ramp into the tug. She pressed the blue stud on the rear wall which caused the ramp to lift up and the hatch to swing down forming a complete enclosure, sealing them in. They traveled the length of the tug's hold until they got to the command section archway which also served as an airlock. Once inside, Rome removed her helmet and Rei did likewise.

"You sit in the pilot's seat, on the left," Rome said pointing there.

"OK," Rei replied and made his way forward and sat down. Rome sat down on the seat to the right.

"Now you buckle yourself in, like so…" She reached behind her and brought one of the two straps over her shoulder. She showed him how to insert the tongue into the hasp. "When it clicks, the latch is fastened."

"Yeah, that's the way our seatbelts worked too."

Rome continued. "We each have a set of controls. OMCOM says you would call them joysticks. They operate differently when the spacecraft is within an atmosphere compared to space."

Rei saw the two sticks, roughly six inches tall, protruding from the very end of the armrests. Each was scalloped as would be required to get the best grip and each had a red button at the top.

"What're the buttons for?" he asked. "Firing weapons?"

"The Vuduri do not use weapons," she said, quite seriously. "We will review the buttons in a bit."

"OK. You're the boss."

"First," she said, "we will cover atmospheric flight. Our principal method of propulsion is the…" Rome paused while OMCOM supplied her with the proper translation. "…the EG lifter pods."

"What does EG stand for?" Rei asked.

"Electrogravity."

"Huh?!" Rei exclaimed. "Electrogravity? What is that?"

"The pods on the underside of the tug create a repulsor field. It provides lift within the lower atmosphere."

"What's a repulsor field?" Rei asked. "I've never…"

Rome interrupted him by holding up her hand. "Let me guess…you have never heard of it."

"Just like everything else around here," Rei said sardonically. "So how do you create one? A repulsor field?"

"We use rotating superconducting magnets to create an antigravity region."

Rei just shook his head. "Here we go again." He took a deep breath. "I know you mentioned plasma thrusters before. If you have antigravity why would you need any other kind of propulsion?"

"The repulsor field only generates lift within a gravity well. It pushes against mass. Its strength tails off in inverse proportion to the distance from the center of the planet. Typically, above an atmosphere, it does not work very well. You could never achieve escape velocity with it. It is just a convenient way to operate on and around a planet."

"Got it," Rei said. "We use the electrogravity superconducting magnetic lifters to take us up. Then what?"

"The button on the left is for the plasma thrusters. They are very powerful so you only use them within an atmosphere if you need to accelerate rapidly."

"Kind of like after-burners, huh? This is just like a fighter jet."

"Perhaps. I am unfamiliar with fighter jets."

"OK, what else?" Rei asked.

Rome showed him how the tug could also use the EG lifters to hover and rotate in place. She pointed to the large flat-panel display taking up most of the front console. "Around the perimeter of the display are all of your instruments. When you want to magnify one, you simply touch it like so..." She reached over and pressed something that looked like a compass. A large replica of the simulated dial appeared in the center of the screen. "And it will center. You can nest, layer or tile multiple displays as needed. You press here," again she reached forward and pressed a section, "to clear the screen and reset."

"It's just like the rest of your displays."

"Yes. Once you are high enough and the EG lifters are no longer effective, the controls switch from atmospheric to space-borne. The trim-jets come into play. For example, pushing the right stick forward fires the rear trim-jets and moves the craft forward. Pulling back does the reverse. You throttle the plasma thrusters to full power by pushing forward on the left stick and down to the minimum by pulling back. It is just the opposite of the EG lifters."

"I'm pretty familiar with this part," Rei said. "Back on Earth, I was a pilot, among other things."

"Yes, I know," Rome said, pointing to her head. "Let us see just how knowledgeable you are. And be aware that there will be some buffeting as we climb through the atmosphere so keep a firm grip on the controls."

"I'll do that. Ready?"

"You will need to verbally instruct OMCOM to open the hangar doors," Rome replied. "It would be very uncomfortable to have to fly through them."

Rei looked over at her and saw that she was smiling. "OK. OMCOM, open the hangar doors, please," Rei said, laughing gently.

"Of course," replied OMCOM from a grille built into the control deck. "I must check for any crew first, please wait... All clear."

Rei felt a vibration as the massive hangar doors pulled open allowing him to look at the surface of Dara for the first time. The ground was brown and reddish, illuminated by the lights of the hangar bay.

"Look at that," Rei said, pointing forward. "For some reason, I was expecting it to be all gray and cratered, like Earth's moon."

"No, Dara has sufficient atmosphere to have weather," Rome said. "That is why we picked it. It reduces the engineering requirements that we'd need for a vacuum. Plus during re-entry we can use aero-braking. That only works if you have an atmosphere to rub against. You may proceed."

"Here goes nuthin'," Rei said, wrapping his hands around the joysticks. "Wait. What about the landing struts?"

Rome replied, "They are activated by proximity sensors. They raise and lower automatically."

"OK." Rei pulled back ever so gently on the left stick. With the tiniest of jolts, the tug shuddered and silently rose into the air. Rei pushed the stick forward and the tug settled back on the ground again.

"That was easy," he said.

Rome did not say a word. She just pointed forward.

Rei pulled back on the left stick again. When they were about six feet off the hangar floor, Rei pulled back on the right stick and the tug began to move toward the giant hangar doors.

Rei smiled. "I don't feel anything. This is really sleek!"

Rome nodded and Rei guided them out of the hangar doors and over the surface of Dara. When they were a sufficient distance from the star-base, Rei pulled back harder on both sticks and the nose of the ship lifted at an ever-increasing angle with ever-increasing speed. When they were nearly vertical, Rei eased back on the right stick, but kept the left one pulled all the way back. Soon, they were flying through the wispy thin cloud layer of Dara. When they were above the clouds, Rome nodded and Rei pressed the button to ignite the plasma drive. Immediately, they were pushed back in their seats. Before long, the curvature of the moon became readily apparent. They continued climbing until they were 200 kilometers above the surface. At that point, Rome had him level off.

She looked down at the instruments. "Orbital velocity achieved. We are good." She held up her hand. "You may shut down the engines for now."

Rei complied. "Hey," he asked. "How come we aren't weightless?"

"When we close the shields, the backwash from the EG lifters produces a low-level of artificial gravity."

"Sleek," Rei said, admiringly.

Rome unbuckled herself and said, "We need to release the probes. Please put on your helmet."

"OK," Rei said, following her lead. They put on their helmets and made their way back to the far end of the cargo compartment. Rome handed Rei a tether and showed him where to attach it on his suit then she pointed to the cargo hatch controls. Rei pressed the blue stud. He could feel the pressure suit stiffening as pumps withdrew the air. When the indicator turned red, the cargo hatch rose up and they were looking at the airless void of interplanetary space.

Rei found the experience to be a little unnerving even with the tether, but the artificial gravity was strong enough that he was able to convince himself that they would not go flying off into space. Together, they unlatched the fifteen or so tubs holding the starprobes. One by one, they removed the lid then pushed the tubs out the back. As each tub was released, a thick cloud issued out of it and began moving off. It took a little while but finally they were done and after resealing the cargo compartment, they returned to the cockpit.

"Now what?" Rei asked as he was buckling in.

"It will take OMCOM quite a while to calibrate all these probes," Rome said. "I want you to practice a jump." Rome pointed forward. "The procedure works best when we are away from any significant gravity wells."

"Why?"

Rome took her hands and formed them into a ball. "You understand the basic principle of forming a PPT tunnel. We need to create a concentrated collection of negative energy."

"Yeah, I got that," Rei said. "I still don't believe it but go on."

"Thank you," Rome said. "The conditions for forming the most stable PPT tunnel require that we come nearly to a halt. Ideally, we want a relative velocity of zero. So we need to be far enough away from a gravity well that we don't start moving in the wrong direction. The first place that the projectors cross pins the entrance to the tunnel. Then we inject more negative energy to extend it, like inflating a balloon. If we are moving, it is harder to stabilize and your tunnel cannot reach as far."

"If you say so."

Rome used the plasma thrusters to accelerate until they achieved escape velocity. The star named Tabit was directly ahead. Rome pointed to the gravitometer. Rei watched the value slowly drift downwards. When it crossed a yellow line, Rome spoke up.

"We are far enough that we can make our jump," she said. "We can have the nav-computer execute the stop turn automatically."

"Stop turn?" Rei asked.

"Yes," Rome replied. "To create the longest PPT tunnel, we need to come to a complete stop. Normally, we turn the ship around and use the plasma thrusters as retrorockets to accomplish this."

"I know I heard you say it before but it's just now sinking in. You're saying that to go faster than the speed of light, we have to come to a dead stop?"

"Yes," Rome replied.

"Doesn't that seem a little goofy to you? Shouldn't we be going really, really fast?"

"It may not seem efficient but it is effective. Using this method, we get to travel at many multiples of the speed of light. Would you not agree that is a desirable goal?"

"Of course but I still think there has to be a better way."

"We do have a static tunnel between Earth and Rogal Canduro, you call it Alpha Centauri."

"That's a hell of a tunnel," Rei observed.

"It is not one long tunnel," Rome replied. "There are a series of relay rings that produce the same net effect."

"Even so, that's more like it," Rei said. "I bet that gets you there fast."

"It does," Rome replied, "however, many Vuduri find it excruciating."

"Why?"

"As I told you earlier, there is so much gravitic radiation from the PPT tunnel generators, if you are not wearing a T-suppressor, it typically renders a Vuduri unconscious."

"So they wear T-suppressors. What's wrong with that?"

"Most Vuduri find being cut off from the Overmind intolerable, even for a short time."

Rei started to make a comment but changed his mind. "I'll take your word for it," he said. "What do we do first?"

"This is the symbol for that sequence." Rome pointed to a flared cone symbol on the front display panel.

"I see it," Rei said.

"Go ahead," Rome said. "Press it."

Rei pressed the symbol and the nav-computer fired the side trim-jets to rotate the tug about its center axis in the horizontal plane. As they did so, Tabit went out of view and Skyler's World became a dominating presence in front of them. Once they were facing exactly back to the direction they came, the opposing trim-jets fired and the rotation stopped. The plasma thrusters came on and Rei watched their relative velocity decrease until it reached zero. Immediately, the nav-computer shut down the engines. As the last part of the maneuver, the nav-computer fired the trim-jets again until they were once more facing Tabit.

"I get it," Rei said. "Now what?"

"Look on the front part of the right armrest," Rome said, pointing. Rei leaned forward. "Do you see the yellow dial with the button in the middle?"

"Yes," Rei answered.

"The outer dial controls the diameter of the tunnel. Normally we just leave it in the center position which is calibrated for this ship. That will change when we begin our journey since our mass will be vastly different."

Rei nodded while Rome continued. "The button in the center activates the PPT projectors. You can press it part way to create a short-throw tunnel or you can press it all the way in until it locks to create the longest tunnel."

"Why do you need a separate control?" Rei asked. "Can't the nav-computer create the tunnel?"

"Yes," Rome said. "But it is the same as with the hand controls. The dial and button bypass the nav-computer. They are there when human judgment is required. For your first jump, I wanted you to do it manually so you get a feel for it."

"OK," Rei said. "So what do I do?"

"Check your outer dial and confirm that the raised indicator is perfectly vertical."

Rei looked at it and saw a tiny triangle pointing straight up. "OK, it's correct."

"Now press the button. For our first jump, just push it in about three quarters of the way."

"Roger," Rei said. He pressed the button in and immediately heard a high-pitched whine emanating from the rear of the ship.

"Is that the PPT generators?" Rei asked.

"Yes. Look out the front."

Rei found it very difficult to see anything through the cockpit windows. He squinted and craned his neck forward. In front of the ship, an ever-widening, nearly pitch-black circle became evident. Actually, it was less that there was a circle as much as it was the absence of tiny points of light. Rome held her hand up while she studied the readouts built into the front display panel. After a short interval, she lowered her hand which Rei took to mean it was enough. He released the PPT activator and pressed the throttle to fire the plasma thrusters. The ship eased forward. Rei watched in wonder as they passed through the dark circle but he felt no sensation other than the acceleration due to the engines. As soon as they were through, Rome told him to release the throttle. The plasma thrusters cut out and they coasted forward.

Rei look up and around. "Did we do it? Where's Tabit?" he asked.

"Behind us," Rome replied. "Here," she said and took over the controls, twisting the navigation stick, rotating the tug so that it was facing the harsh glow of Tabit which now stood in front of them once again. The glint of the star reflected off the nose of the tug.

"How is that possible? We never entered a tunnel," Rei noted.

"The word tunnel is meant figuratively, not literally. It is not like a tunnel on Earth," Rome replied. "The word tunnel is from a perspective outside the ship. From inside, the tunnel would appear infinitely thin."

"I still would have expected something," Rei said. "Does your bloco and stilo work out here?"

"Insofar as it receives data from the on-board computer. Not from OMCOM," Rome said, "not from this distance."

"So do you know how far we jumped?" he asked Rome.

She closed her eyes for a second then said, "approximately one hundred light minutes."

"What!?" Rei said. "That's like…" Rei tried to do the math in his head. "Uh, over a billion kilometers?"

"Yes, that is a good guess. In fact, the actual distance we traveled is a bit over 1.8 billion kilometers."

"That's incredible," Rei said. "Almost 2 billion kilometers in no time at all. I felt absolutely nothing."

Rome smiled.

"So where's Skyler's World?" Rei asked.

Rome pointed to a section of the window. "It is that bright point, right there."

Rei squinted and saw a tiny point of light that was a bit brighter than those around it. He was stunned. "This is absolutely unbelievable," he blurted out. "We'll be at Tau Ceti in no time!"

Rome's smile dimmed a bit. "No, we only traveled 100 light minutes. For us to go to Deucado, we must traverse 21 light *years*. Towing your Ark, it will take us two years to go that distance."

Quietly, he said, "You're right. It's kind of hard to realize. It's gonna be a long haul, isn't it?"

"Yes, it is," she replied. "But at least it is doable." She pointed toward Skyler's World. "Do you think you can take us home?"

"Yes ma'am," Rei said. "Can I do the stop turn manually?"

"Of course," Rome answered. "Just be careful."

They were already facing away from their forward vector so it only took a few bursts from the plasma thrusters to bring their relative velocity down to zero. Like a seasoned veteran, Rei used his prior experience to generate the PPT tunnel and push them through.

Appearing out of nowhere, Skyler's World loomed in front of him like a gigantic version of Jupiter. From this vantage point, the astonishing gas giant was magnificently gaudy with bands of blue, brown, red and tan plus uncounted swirling portions of white, silver and cyan. On the base below, beneath the thin atmosphere, the World appeared redder, shining over half the heavens. Up here, it looked dazzlingly closer and more forbidding, filling the entire sky with its disorienting complexities. To Rei, it made the ground seem a half million kilometers straight down. Rei tried to imagine the unthinkable pressures that crushed its surface into a howling chemical slush.

"Very good," Rome said, lifting Rei from his reverie. "That is it for now. It is time to return to the base. We will let the nav-computer land the vessel. Reentering the atmosphere is not the kind of thing we can have you practice without demonstrating it once."

"I heartily agree," Rei said.

Rome took the controls and adjusted their vector so that they pointed directly at Dara. She pressed the thruster lock until they were close enough. After she released it, she programmed the nav-computer to circularize their orbit using the trim-jets. When she was satisfied with the data entry, she pressed the execute button. Immediately, the plasma thrusters roared to life pressing Rei and Rome back into their seats.

"No!" Rome shouted. She stabbed at the icon to cancel the maneuver but nothing happened.

"What's going on?" Rei asked, alarmed at Rome's reaction.

Rome ignored him. She grabbed the control sticks pressing the thruster buttons off and on repeatedly. They continued to accelerate.

"Rome?" Rei asked breathlessly.

Steely-faced, Rome turned toward him. "The plasma thrusters should not be on. There is a malfunction or cross-circuit. We are accelerating toward the moon. We need to decelerate. Try your controls. Guide us away."

Rei pulled on his control sticks but there was no reaction. He stabbed at the thruster lock. It was lifeless.

"OMCOM?" Rome called out.

"I am here. Why are you accelerating?" the computer answered through the grille built into the front of the cockpit.

"The nav-computer is not responding to orders," Rome answered. "It fired the thrusters. I cannot shut them off. Can you stop it?"

After a few seconds, OMCOM replied, "I cannot contact the nav-computer. It is locked into a tight loop. I triggered the non-maskable interrupt but its execution cycling will not stop. You will need to shut it down and restart it for me to reestablish communications."

"We are already in the exosphere," Rome said. "How much time will that take?"

"No more than three minutes," OMCOM replied.

"Three minutes!" Rome exclaimed. "We will be in the mesosphere by then. We will burn up."

"These are the facts," OMCOM said. "The nav-computer has locked out the manual controls as well. You must shut it down to regain control."

Rome's eyes grew wider and wider. She turned toward Rei. All the color had left her face and she just shook her head from side to side.

"Can you pull up?" Rei asked quietly.

"We no longer have any control," Rome answered softly, her face locked in mask of helplessness.

Chapter 15

IT HAD BEEN REI'S EXPERIENCE THAT STARING DEATH IN THE FACE has a way of sobering you up. First there was the airlock incident and now this. Slamming into Dara appeared to be their only fate but Rei was determined not to die. He looked down and spotted the yellow PPT dial. He snapped his head back up and looked over at Rome.

"Can you fire up the PPT generators?" he asked.

"What?" Rome sputtered. "Why would you want to do that?"

"What if we could jump past the moon? That would give you more than enough time to reboot your computer."

"We are moving too fast and we are too far into the gravity well," Rome replied grimly. "A PPT tunnel would not form."

"Actually, it would," OMCOM interjected. "It will not project very far but my simulation says it would be far enough."

"What?" Rome asked. "What about the gravity well? What about our velocity?"

"Make the widest possible tunnel. Enough negative energy will accumulate to jump you a short distance, at least the diameter of Dara," the computer offered.

"Will it remain open long enough?" Rome asked desperately.

"Yes. Just keep the projectors on until you are through the tunnel. Do not let up like normal."

"I have never heard of such a thing," Rome said.

OMCOM pointed out, "That is because no one would ever do such a thing. However, that does not mean it will not work,"

"Can you do it, Romey?" Rei asked.

"We can try," Rome answered. She rotated the outer dial on the PPT switch to generate the largest possible tunnel then she pushed down on the center stud to activate the PPT generators. Their high-pitched whine infiltrated the cockpit. Rome pressed as hard as she could. A dark circle formed in front of them, occluding a small portion of the moon. They closed in very quickly. There was a dark flash and the moon was gone. The only thing in front of them was interplanetary space.

Rei craned his head around, looking out the side window and confirmed that Dara was behind them. "Woo hoo," Rei shouted. "We did it."

"Yes, we did," Rome said, smiling broadly. "That was amazing!" She took her finger off the PPT activator and sank back into her seat for a moment.

"Now what?" Rei asked, feeling the thrust of the plasma thrusters continuing.

"We shut it down," Rome said. She straightened up then unbuckled. She climbed down to the floor, reaching up underneath the control deck and removed a panel built into the control console. She felt around until she found the interlock. She pulled it and the viewscreens went dark. Immediately, the plasma thrusters shut down. Rome waited about ten seconds then reset the switch. The viewscreens came back on and showed a steady march of diagnostic symbols indicating startup. Rome snapped the panel back in place and took her seat.

"Can you get us back?" Rei asked.

"If we can get the manual controls to respond," Rome said. She pressed a series of buttons and restarted the initialization sequence allowing the system to reboot normally. Rome had OMCOM run a diagnostic on every subsystem within the tug. She was pleased to see that the reboot procedure seemed to have done the trick. OMCOM confirmed her findings. The computer found evidence of one anomaly which somehow erased itself during the restart. With all systems checked out, Rome tested the manual controls and found they responded as expected. She swung the ship around and used the plasma thrusters to reverse their course and reenter orbit around Dara. When that was done, she sat back in her seat again.

"What?" Rei asked.

"Nothing," Rome said. "I just need a moment to compose myself. I do not trust the nav-computer to land us. I will do it manually."

"Take your time," Rei said, considering the alternative.

Rome took a deep breath and rotated the ship to use the plasma thrusters in retro mode. A short burst was all it took then she rotated them forward again. They passed through the thermosphere and the

EG lifters engaged. The lifters pushed against the gravity of the planet retarding their forward speed but not nearly enough to prevent the forces of friction from heating up the nose. As they entered the mesosphere, the hull temperature shot up. When the temperature hit the critical value, Rome cycled the EG lifters to raise the nose and they headed upwards again back toward space. Their relative velocity slowed and the excess heat dissipated into the thin upper reaches of the atmosphere. They nearly stalled but this was part of the plan. Their arc did not take them nearly as high as they were before. Once again, Rome aimed the nose of the ship downward and they reentered the atmosphere, deeper still this time. Again, when enough heat had built up, Rome swooped upward. Using this method, it only took five dips to slow them down sufficiently to where they remained fully within the atmosphere with a tolerable forward speed. Rome headed toward the station.

Rei looked out the window at the airfoil to his left. His inner engineer prompted him to ask, "Those wings don't look very aerodynamic. Do they provide much lift?"

"No, none at all. They are strictly for control. The EG pods provide all the lift we need. The trim-jets do not work very well within an atmosphere. Otherwise, we would not need the wings at all."

Soon they were approaching the base. Rome circled around once and Rei saw the Vuduri starship called the Algol for the first time. Unlike the boxier tugs, this spaceship was a graceful white presence, smooth, shaped like a tapered hourglass with large wings and thruster pods mounted on the wingtips.

"Wow," he said. "That is some kind of starship."

Rome looked where Rei was staring and said, "Yes, it is beautiful, is it not? I had never noticed before. It was much larger, longer actually, when we first came here. We had additional cargo bays mounted on the back but now you see its true form."

After they completed their circle, Rome requested that OMCOM open the hangar doors. At this point, Rome turned the controls over to Rei. Under her watchful eye, Rei guided the tug into the spaceport until it was fully enclosed. He brought it to a complete stop inside the hangar, hovering in place. Twisting the control stick caused the tug to rotate about its midpoint so that it was facing outwards, ready for its next sortie. He landed with nary a bump. They put on their helmets and exited the craft via the rear cargo ramp.

Once they were inside the Iso chamber, they took off their helmets. Rome had a great big smile on her face.

"You did a very good job," she said. "And your idea saved us."

"Thanks," Rei replied, smiling broadly. "Just a regular day at the office. So what's next? Do we need to tell somebody about the malfunction?"

"OMCOM already knows. I need to see how he is doing with those probes."

"OK," Rei said, sitting down on the bench.

Rome wriggled out of her pressure suit and was pulling on her jumpsuit when she turned to look at Rei who was sitting there, half stripped down. He was staring at her, his head tilted slightly to the side.

"What?" she asked.

"Did you know that you are absolutely gorgeous?" he opined.

Rome smiled. "You are just saying that because you are in love with me. I am actually quite ordinary."

"You're wrong and I can prove it!"

"How?"

"Have you ever heard the expression 'beauty is in the eye of the beholder'?" Rei asked.

"No," said Rome.

"Do you understand it though?"

"Of course," replied Rome. "It means that beauty is subjective and measured according to the perception and parameters of the observer."

"Exactly," Rei said. "So, that means you don't get to be the judge. I do. And if I say you're beautiful, then you are beautiful. Case closed!"

"Well that is very nice. Thank you," Rome said. "Now please get changed. We must get back to the observatory."

While Rome and Rei were in space, OMCOM had been calibrating the millions and millions of starprobes. Once Rome had arrived, the computer showed her the results of those calibrations. As a demonstration, he took the massively parallel array first toward Skyler's World then away accelerating at what appeared to be an inconceivable velocity. Rome used the test to prepare her recording apparatus. OMCOM did a fly-by of the other planets within the star system, exercising the microwave and IR detectors in addition to the visible light sensors.

"I think he's enjoying this," Rei observed as he watched Rome's hands flying over the workstation input surface, getting ready for the broadcast.

"Of course," she replied. "It is a virtual time machine. OMCOM is now free to explore the universe. Why would he not enjoy it?"

The image was soaring, flickering in and out as OMCOM sent the view around and around an orbit just outside of Skyler's World. The planet flew by a dizzying speed.

"Enough play time," said Commander Ursay to OMCOM. "Can you go to the wavefront?"

"Of course," replied OMCOM. "I will start prior to the disappearance."

Within a few minutes, a tiny point appeared centered within the image. The point of light grew and grew until Winfall became a discernible disk. The star continued to grow until it occupied most of the viewscreen.

"I have compensated for the brightness so that you are seeing a normalized view."

"All right," Ursay said. "When was this image taken?"

"17 years ago. I am going to move forward in time until we can observe the occlusion event."

The disk remained frozen in the center of the screen. At first, Rei found it hard to tell what was going on. He had to remind himself that this was incredible, that there were millions of microscopic probes jumping in and out of range at speeds so far beyond the speed of light and yet the image they were seeing looked like it came from a movie projector.

Finally, Winfall started to dim. Unlike a normal eclipse, this one appeared to be moving from the top and the bottom of the star at the same time. The high resolution display allowed them to see that the edges were straight rather than rounded. Rei peered intently trying to envision the process but it was hard to make out what was happening.

"I am going to go backwards in time a bit and see if I can focus on whatever is causing the dimming," OMCOM announced.

The virtual camera snapped back in time and the eclipse started over again. As before, the edges of the eclipse were straight and reminded Rei of a shutter closing. They watched as the dark regions at the top and bottom approached each other until the star disappeared.

"Zoom back more," Ursay commanded OMCOM. "See if you can capture around the star."

OMCOM went backwards in time yet again. The bright yellow disk was once again the whole star. OMCOM shifted the virtual camera to the left and pulled back so that the star was now on the right.

"Look there," Rei said, pointing to the left side of Winfall. "All the stars to the left are occluded even now."

"Som," Ursay muttered.

"Nothing to the right, all looks normal," Rome added. She pressed some icons on her display. "Switching to multi-spectrum," she said.

The occlusion which had appeared pitch black was rendered into a false-color image of mottled browns and dark red with black blotches.

"Zoom back farther," Ursay insisted. "Keep going until you can see stars all around the occlusion."

The virtual camera pulled back farther and farther. Winfall shrank until it was just a large dot on the screen. Finally, when the camera pulled back far enough, they could see that the thing to the left was spherical but a sphere so large its volume was nearly inconceivable.

"OMCOM," Rome said in a shaky voice, "how big is that? What is the diameter?"

"Roughly 1.5 light minutes across. Approximately 35 million kilometers."

"Whoa," Rei said. He knew the Sun was only 1.4 million kilometers across. This thing was more than 20 times larger than that. The concept was mind-boggling.

The virtual camera stopped panning back and the three humans watched the right edge of the sphere. A split developed along its equator. Stars in the background could be seen in the gap between the two halves. The gap continued to grow wider and wider. The pivot point was roughly mid-sphere. Perhaps one-eighth of the circumference was in motion. The entire sphere started moving to the right, its trajectory causing the gap to move in on Winfall. Before their eyes, in the reflected light of the star, they saw Winfall enter a kind of hollow chamber until it was completely enveloped. Then the gap closed. The star was gone. To Rei, it looked exactly like a cosmic Pac-Man. Once the gap was closed, the only thing remaining was the absence of stars mid-screen. It was as if Winfall never existed.

The three humans were stunned into silence. Finally, Ursay said, "Asdrale Cimatir" in a hoarse whisper.

"What did he say?" Rei asked Rome.

"He calls it a Stareater," said Rome gravely.

Chapter 16

NO ONE SPOKE FOR THE LONGEST TIME. EVERYONE JUST STOOD there, staring up at the impossible image on the screen.

"Jesus," said Rei. "How can that be?"

"I do not know," Rome answered, barely breathing, "I have never seen anything like it."

"Again," Ursay commanded, finally.

OMCOM complied. It was just as horrible the second time as the first. The thing literally swallowed the star whole.

"Pull back farther," Ursay insisted.

OMCOM pulled back and they stared at it, trying to understand that which was incomprehensible.

Rei pointed and said, "Look, there. On the far side."

"What do you see?" Rome asked.

"There's something there, something different."

The virtual camera went swooping down. As it approached, they could see that the Stareater had bands across its surface, like a gas giant but staggeringly larger. And like a gigantic planet, it had mountains and valleys. Crisscrossing its entire surface were regular features that looked like pillboxes or crossbeams. They could see craters. All in all, it was a bewildering mix of the artificial and the natural.

"Who could have built such a thing?" Rome asked, "and why?"

"There is no way to tell," OMCOM replied.

Rei turned to her and said, "I don't know that much about it, but back in the middle of the 20th century, a physicist by the name of Freeman Dyson proposed that the most efficient way to capture the energy generated by a star was to encase it in a giant sphere. I guess somebody went ahead and built one."

"But why? Surely they know that…" Rome said, not even able to formulate a proper question.

The virtual viewpoint began to focus in. Despite the fact that there was incredible detail, beyond a certain point, like fractals, it was all the same.

"There," Rei said, pointing. "OMCOM, what is that bump toward the back?"

OMCOM did not reply, but the virtual point of view panned across until a protrusion centered in the screen.

"Can you zoom in?" Ursay asked.

"Of course," OMCOM replied.

The bump became larger. The protuberance was spherical in nature and looked like it was grafted on, almost like a boil. Its surface resembled that of the much larger sphere.

"Bring us forward in time, slowly," Ursay commanded.

"Advancing."

The image stayed rock steady, but just like a balloon being inflated with a pump, the small protrusion became larger and larger until it was almost one quarter of the size of the Stareater. The object shuddered and then it disconnected from the larger sphere and moved off. In a wink, it was gone.

"What did we just see?" Rei asked.

"I will reverse the image and review it at a slower speed," OMCOM said.

The smaller sphere suddenly reappeared, once again attached to the larger one.

"Forward," OMCOM announced.

As before, it disconnected and moved off, but this time far more slowly. As it began to move forward, they could see a pitch black circle appear in front of it. The circle grew and grew until it was larger than the sphere itself. The sphere moved toward the circle and then began disappearing in slow motion, swallowed up by the black region. To Rei, it looked as if something were slicing off the lead edge or else moving through an invisible wall.

"What is that?" Rome asked.

"What does the entrance to a PPT tunnel look like from the other end?" Rei asked. "Around the back, I mean."

"It would look like nothing out of the ordinary. The tunnel only affects the ship projecting it."

"So wouldn't it look just like that?" Rei asked, pointing at the projected display.

"You are saying the Stareater just stepped through a PPT tunnel?" Rome exclaimed with horror.

"Nei bita sar," said Ursay.

"Think about it," Rei said. "These things travel at an average velocity around one half c. They need time to build a baby. So the only way the little one can keep up that speed is if they have FTL capacity when the time comes."

"Why do you say, 'baby'?" Rome asked.

"What else would you call it?" Rei replied.

"Ni, ni," said Ursay. "Nei a bissofal." He just looked down, shaking his head.

OMCOM sped up the passage of time and they could see that the original sphere was swelling in size. When it had just about doubled, it suddenly disappeared and the background field of stars shone through as though nothing had happened other than the absence of Winfall.

"Fe bere dres, fe bere dres," Ursay shouted. "Go back."

The large sphere reappeared and this time OMCOM moved forward much more slowly. Once again, they could see a gigantic black spot appear and the monstrous creature went through it and was gone.

"These things just eat stars and move on," Rei said, suddenly feeling exhausted. He closed his eyes.

"OMCOM," Rome said. "How is it possible to eat a star? Would not the corona burn up inside? Would not the pressure cause the sphere to explode?"

"Obviously not," OMCOM said. "The empirical evidence is in front of us. Perhaps once the Stareater has siphoned off the outer photosphere, the remaining thermonuclear reaction dies down. There may not be much outward pressure at all. It would then digest the remaining matter and perhaps that is the source of the material to allow it to grow."

"Grow?" Rome said helplessly, "and then what?"

"I would assume it moves off in search of another star to consume."

"OMCOM, where did these things come from?" Rei asked.

"I have insufficient data to draw a conclusion."

"Are there any more, besides the two that we know about?" Rome asked.

"I will look. I will spread the probe array out along this vector. We will lose some resolution, but gain field dispersal."

The image of the Stareater was replaced by a star field as the virtual camera moved past its previous position. The resolution diminished as OMCOM spread the starprobes out, spanning an incalculable distance. A flash occurred and then faded.

"What was that?" Rei asked.

"That was a star that had been previously visible and now is gone. I am logging its position as a possible locus for another Stareater."

There was another flash. No one said a word this time. There was another flash and another. The sequence became a steady stream. The frequency and density of the flashes kept increasing. Rei felt sick to his stomach. There was no real way to comprehend the magnitude of what they were seeing.

"I have completed my mapping as far as I can go," OMCOM said. "However, I must offer this caveat. I have only searched along a single vector. We can assume there would be other occurrences in other directions. There may even be some close by. I have no way of knowing without performing essentially a galactic sweep."

"Show us what you plotted so far," said Ursay, hoarsely.

Rising above the plane of the ecliptic, a symbolic representation of the arms of the galaxy became noticeable. A bright yellow region appeared that followed the decreased density of stars between the spiral arms of the Milky Way. Rei asked himself, if the Stareaters were responsible for the gaps between arms, every galaxy had them, it would mean... He couldn't get his brain to go beyond that thought.

"How many of them are there?" Rome whispered.

"My probes are limited in number. This is just an estimate. It is possible that some of the stars disappeared for other reasons. But so far I have detected more than one thousand."

All three humans gasped at the same time.

"The stars themselves vary in type and diameter. There is a weak correlation in size and distance which may indicate that some of the Stareaters, perhaps the larger ones, travel more slowly."

No one made a sound. During the silence, OMCOM drew in first one line then another until he had constructed a wire-frame around the swarm. The computer shaded the drawing until it became roughly conical. The view projected onto the sphere became more symbolic. Within the display, there were numbers and coordinates that began to change. OMCOM slowly advanced the cone of destruction forward until the tip touched a yellow icon with a red ring around it, ever expanding.

"Oh, no," Rei uttered, sadly.

"Yes," said OMCOM. "My original estimate stands. If the swarm continues upon its current path and velocity, it will hit Earth in less than three years. Earth cannot survive an encounter with even one of these creatures much less a group."

"Are they targeting Earth specifically?" Rome asked in a hushed tone.

"Does it matter?" OMCOM replied cryptically.

No one could speak after that. Several other crewmen including one woman came over to gawk at the display, but no one said a word. Rome, who was standing by now, moved next to Rei and took his hand. Rei could feel her shivering so he released her hand and put his arm around her waist.

The ghastly sight just sat there, the bright yellow region and the bullseye painted on Earth. The whole situation was just so wrong. After a long moment of silence, all the crewmen moved quickly and purposefully out of Stellar Cartography, leaving only Ursay, Rei and Rome remaining.

"We are abandoning this base. Now!" Commander Ursay said firmly and moved to walk out of the room.

Chapter 17

"HOLD ON A SEC," REI SHOUTED AFTER HIM. "WHY ARE YOU abandoning the base? Don't we need to find out more?"

Ursay turned back to him. "We must get this information to Earth," Ursay said.

"Why?" Rei asked insistently.

"Because?" said Ursay shaking his head. "Did you not just see? Because there is a creature or creatures headed toward Earth that will destroy it."

"So what good does it do to tell them?"

"I do not understand what you are saying," Ursay said, scowling. "This is the end of all life. We must warn them. They must abandon the Solar System."

"And go where?" Rei asked, again, insistently.

"Why, somewhere else. Somewhere out of the path of the thing," Ursay said, exasperated.

"What good will that do?"

"What do you mean? Why do you keep asking me these things?" Ursay sputtered. "Informing Earth, it will save the people. What is wrong with you to even question this?"

"Yes, you'll save some people for now. But how long will that last?" Rei replied. "You saw how many there are. No matter where you go, they're going to find you and destroy the stars."

"So what do you suggest?" Ursay spat out.

"Fight back," Rei offered.

"How?" Rome asked, shocked.

"There is not enough firepower in the entire world that would make a dent in a creature of that size," Ursay said. "Even if we took all the weapons of your age plus all previous ages and applied them all at once, it would not even slow it down."

"What about anti-matter?" Rei asked. "Can you guys make some of that?"

Ursay just sighed. "To create enough antimatter to attack just one, with our current production capability... OMCOM, how long?"

"Using current technology, it would take a minimum of 150 years. And there is no known way to store such a large quantity."

131

"You see?" Ursay said, "We do not have enough time. There is no way."

"So find a way then. You can't just let it go unchallenged." Rei said.

"How?" Ursay croaked.

"Rei, perhaps you should tell them about H. G. Wells," OMCOM offered.

"Which book?" Rei asked.

"War of the Worlds."

Rei squinted, then opened his eyes wide. "You're right, OMCOM!"

"What is it?" Rome asked.

"I know you guys don't have fiction, but we did when I was growing up. One of the genres I loved reading was called science fiction which was speculation about possible futures."

"How is this relevant?" Ursay asked. "The Overmind is familiar with the reference, but cannot see how it applies."

"Well, there was a classic story, written in the 19th century by a man named H. G. Wells. The book was called 'War of the Worlds.' It was about an invasion of Earth by malevolent creatures from Mars."

Rome just shook her head slowly. "Rei, there is no life on Mars," she said to him in a didactic tone.

"Yes, I know, dear. That's why it was called science *fiction*."

"Go on," said Ursay.

"Anyway, the creatures from Mars were all-powerful. No Earth weapons could touch them and it looked like they were going to conquer the planet and destroy all of humanity."

"So did they?" asked Rome.

"No. They were defeated," Rei replied.

"How!?" Ursay insisted.

"By bacteria," Rei answered. "They got sick and died."

"So you are proposing that we send bacteria to make the Stareaters sick? How would such a thing be possible?" Ursay asked, exasperated.

"Not bacteria," Rei answered, sounding distant. He turned to address the grille. "So, OMCOM? Are you saying that you can make actual gray goo?" Rei asked.

"Of course," OMCOM replied.

"Qua?" Ursay asked.

"Gray goo," Rei said. "Nanites, nanobots, whatever you call them now. Self-replicating. Slime that eats everything in sight. It grows forever. It's the power of the exponent."

"Rei, where would we get these?" Rome asked.

"We already have them," OMCOM said. "It would be a simple matter to reprogram the starprobe foundries to achieve the desired results."

OMCOM replaced the projection of the Milky Way with a positron micrograph of the foundry fabrication process.

"Their Casimir pumps make them self-sustaining. We would modify them so that they would have no purpose other than creating more units. I will hard-code the instructions into the units themselves. They will replicate without bound. If we can figure out some way to deliver these units to a Stareater, they would simply consume it."

"It will take too long," Ursay said.

"On the contrary," OMCOM replied. "It will not take long at all."

On the dome, OMCOM projected a series of numbers. "Assume that you start with one thousand one nanogram units. These units should be able to reproduce themselves within three minutes. At the end of the three minutes, you would have two thousand units. At the end of six minutes, you would have four thousand units and so on. Within six hours, the total mass of such a system would be, in theory, equal to that of the Moon. Thirty minutes later, it would achieve the mass of the Earth. Continued unabated, one and one half hours later, it would achieve the mass of the Sun."

"How will they stand up to their own weight? Won't they crush themselves after there are too many?" Rei asked.

OMCOM replied. "I will revise their two-dimensional structure to handle a gravitational stress much larger than that presented by the Stareater."

"Give us the plans," said Ursay. "Whether it works or not, we will transmit this information to Earth."

"You should allow me to build you some prototypes now," OMCOM said.

"Why?" asked Rome.

"It is not my intention to alarm you any further," said OMCOM, "but to be perfectly frank, I can foresee several scenarios where you would either need to have them ready or at least available to study."

"How long before you can have these things ready?" Rei asked.

OMCOM replied, "Assuming you agree, I can have many thousands of prototypes ready within one half hour."

"One half hour," Ursay exclaimed. "To build these, these things?"

"They need a name," Rei interjected. "I think we should call them VIRUS units."

"Where did you come up with that?" Rome asked.

"In my day, we were big on acronyms. So I just figured they are virtually identical replicating unit systems, ergo, VIRUS." Rei said.

"Very clever," OMCOM observed. "Commander Ursay, should I proceed?"

"OMCOM, what would happen if one of these units got loose here?" Rome asked. "Would it not begin to consume whatever it touched?"

"I have already anticipated that. I will design in an oxygen detector. This will guarantee that they will not replicate in an environment where the oxygen concentration is above, say 10%. That would protect the Earth, for example, should any units get loose there."

"That will suffice," Ursay said. "You may proceed."

"Even if you build them, how do you get these VIRUS units to the Stareater?" Rei asked.

"Currently, I do not have a methodology," OMCOM replied. "However, I am certain that they will be able to design a delivery system on Earth that can transport and land the units on the Stareater. I can build your prototypes but beyond that, my contribution is limited to acquiring and transmitting information."

Ursay put his hands to his head. He nodded to himself then he looked at Rome. "We must abandon this base and get the information and prototypes to Earth. The tug outfitted with the MINIMCOM unit has already been launched and is docked with Rei's ship. Rome, after you prepare the VIRUS units you are relieved of duty. Make certain that you are satisfied with the supplies loaded on your tug, and then you may leave when ready."

"Cimbraantoti," Rome said. She nodded toward the door.

"Wait," said Ursay, "there is one more thing we wish to say."

"What is it?" Rome asked.

"Rei…" Ursay stepped forward and placed his hand on Rei's shoulder. Rome was stunned at such a gesture. In a low voice, Ursay said, "When we first found you, we presumed you a blight, a burden. You were from Garecei Ti Essessoni. We cast Rome out because we thought you had compromised this woman, with your undisciplined mind, your murderous past. We were going to exile you, but now…"

"Now what?" Rei asked.

"You have demonstrated to us that as an individual, you have worth. That your separateness is of value. It is something we must consider in the future. For this, we thank you."

Rei's face lit up. "Well, you are welcome, sir!" Ursay removed his hand and nodded. Rei and Rome took that as their cue to leave and headed back toward OMCOM's fabrication facility.

"That was so unlike a Vuduri," Rome said as they were walking. "To touch you like that? You have changed this Overmind in a profound fashion."

"Actually, Rome," Rei replied, "I think it's you that has changed them."

"How?"

"In you they see the potential for all Vuduri when they're not controlled so heavily by the Overmind. You're the future, not me."

"Well," Rome said as they entered OMCOM's central store, "let us agree that together, we have given the Overmind much to think about."

"Roger that."

135

Rome took her place in front of the design screen. She watched as OMCOM modified the architecture of the starprobe foundries to suit their new role. At last, the first unit was extruded from the fabricator followed by another and another, the rate of production ever-increasing.

"They look the same as before," Rei said. "What's different about them?"

Rome pointed to one section of the screen. "Here is the read-only memory, which is new. And here," she pointed to a different area, "OMCOM has converted the second Casimir pump into what looks like an auxiliary internal power source to supplement the first one."

Rei nodded like he knew what she was talking about, but he really didn't see a difference.

"And here," she said, pointing to the left, "this must be the solid-state oxygen detector. That will keep the units dormant for now."

"That's a good thing," Rei said.

Rome walked over to a flat surface by the assembly bay and showed Rei the cases that were being built to house the units. She pointed to a little fishbowl in the middle.

"OMCOM created this container. These bowls will hold the VIRUS units. The cases themselves are air-tight so that the oxygen will be retained and the units will remain deactivated until we know what we are going to do with them."

"And once they're loose, when do they turn off?" Rei asked.

"Yes. That is a good point. OMCOM?" Rome inquired. "What is to prevent them from consuming one another and the whole process aborting?"

"I have engineered the units to only draw raw materials from sources other than themselves," OMCOM said. "In this case, it will be the Stareater. Call it an anti-cannibalism directive. Under normal circumstances, they will not consume one another. They will work cooperatively."

"This really will work, won't it?" Rei said, "We're actually going to make these things sick and die! Well, if they were alive, I mean. OMCOM, are the Stareaters alive or are they machines?"

"The difference is academic. They need to be stopped."

"One cannot help but be curious," Rome interjected. "OMCOM, take a guess. Do you think the Stareaters are alive?"

"I am still analyzing the data, so I cannot render a definitive answer at this time. However, after you leave, I will have much time to ponder this and other questions."

"Yeah. Sorry," Rei said. "I feel kind of bad for you. Everyone is leaving you here, holding the bag."

"I am not sure what bag you are referring to, but it is time for you and Rome to go. I have summoned the loading crew. Very shortly, I will have many cases filled with the VIRUS units. The crew can load them aboard the Algol. It is prepped and ready to leave. As Commander Ursay suggested, you should go inspect your new living quarters before it is too late."

Chapter 18

ROME AND REI STOOD TO THE SIDE OF THE GIANT INNER DOOR OF the hangar. In front of them was the tug that was to be their home for the next two years. The Vuduri crew were rushing in and out carrying boxes and building materials and all manner of items that Rei did not recognize. He stood there in awe of how truly large this place was. When the Vuduri first arrived here, there was no hangar, no star-base, nothing but dirt. They built all of this from scratch. And now they were abandoning it. As the various crew members walked by, many of them nodded and some even gently smiled at them offering a stark contrast to the reception Rei received when he first came aboard the station.

"Where'd all these people come from?" Rei asked.

"They have been here," Rome replied.

"How come I never saw any of them before?"

"Most wished to avoid contact with you when you were first revived," Rome said. "This was already explained to you."

"Why is everyone being so friendly now?" Rei asked.

"Commander Ursay explained it to you. The Overmind recognizes that you are responsible for possibly saving all of humanity if not all life in the universe. I think this is its way of showing appreciation."

"Sleek," Rei said, looking up at the ship. "Should we go take a look?"

"Yes. That is a good idea."

Being careful to not get in the way of the crew transporting materials, Rei and Rome made their way up the 30-degree ramp into the cargo compartment of the bright white tug. Except for the rounded roof, Rei couldn't even tell that it was a space vehicle. With its rooms off to either side, the inside reminded him of a double-wide trailer back on Earth.

They walked along the corridor formed by the newly installed compartments taking care to squeeze to the side whenever a worker passed by them. They entered the first doorway they came to, off to the right and Rome squealed in delight.

"What a beautiful bedroom!" she said.

Rei looked around. On the far wall, there was a big bed and spread about the room was furniture complete with a sitting area.

"Wow," Rei exclaimed. "For people who have no need for taste or comfort, this certainly is elaborate."

"I am sure OMCOM had an influence on its design," Rome observed.

Rei turned back and stared at the bed for a moment. He cleared his throat and started to speak but then stopped.

"What?" Rome asked.

"Uh…" Rei stammered. "This is going to sound too clinical but I don't think it would be a good idea if you got pregnant during the trip. We need to figure out something."

"That is not an issue," Rome said. "Vuduri women control when they ovulate. I will not become pregnant unless you and I decide the time is right."

"OK," Rei said, relieved to drop the subject.

They left that room and moved on to the next which was a galley and eating area. That room had several food synthesizers along with appliances that seemed out of place in the 35th century. There was an oven, a stove and a refrigerator. There was also a square table with two chairs.

"I guess they're expecting me to cook for you," Rei said.

"I would certainly hope so," Rome replied. "And you can teach me as well."

"Sure."

The next room they came to was a fully-equipped gymnasium with some equipment that Rei recognized, including an elliptical trainer, but there was more that he did not recognize.

"What's all this for?" he asked.

"Why, exercise, of course," replied Rome. "Two of the three EG lifters will have to be used as magnetic clamps so we will only have one-third gravity. We will have to exercise every day to get ready for Deucado. It has nearly the same gravity as Earth."

"That's good to hear," Rei said.

He and Rome worked their way back, past the mid-ship airlock and storage lockers then entered a living area with a workstation, seating area and some more electronic equipment.

Rei just stood there a moment, trying to formulate a thought. "Rome, what are we going to do every day? It's like being under house arrest."

"What is house arrest?" Rome asked.

"If you do something wrong and the authorities don't want to put you in prison," Rei answered, "they make you stay in your house and they put a security anklet on you that tells them your whereabouts."

"A security anklet? That would be like a tracking bracelet?" Rome asked.

"Yeah, I guess."

"We have those," Rome said. "For the mandasurte, of course. Vuduri would not need those."

"Right," Rei said.

"Why are we discussing house arrest, anyway?" Rome asked.

"You and me, we'll be locked up, really. Two years is a long time to be cooped up in a flying house. Even one as nice as this," Rei said.

"I think there is more that you are not telling me," Rome observed. "Why do you question this?"

"It's nothing. Never mind," he said.

"No, tell me," she replied. "Remember, I cannot read minds anymore."

"OK. I'll tell you. I love you so much that I don't have very good judgment when it comes to this. But, when you think about it logically, even though it feels like I've known you my whole life, we've only really just met. I'd hate to think of us being stuck together and not enjoying it."

"Do not concern yourself with…" Her breath caught, and then her brow furrowed. "Are you worried that we are not meant to be together?" she asked with some concern.

"Oh no, god, no. It isn't that," Rei answered hurriedly. "This has nothing to do with my feelings. It's just an observation, a hypothetical. I mean, how will we end up not going stir crazy if there is nowhere to go and nothing to do for such a long time?"

Rome laughed, relieved. "You are being silly. There will be much to do. You must learn to speak Vuduri. No one on Deucado will take the time to learn English like I did."

"Sure, that makes sense," Rei agreed.

"And you must learn all about Vuduri science, technology, history and more. When we reanimate your people, as you well know, there will be a culture shock and we have to be ready to orient them to the new world."

"I understand," Rei said, shaking his head.

"And there is so much I want to learn about your world," Rome said firmly. "There was much lost after the Great Dying. There is a vast amount of history that you can fill in that will help others to understand exactly what happened. After today, I am sure the Vuduri will find it of interest."

"OK. What else?" Rei asked.

"OMCOM tells me he had them include art supplies, music generators…oh!"

"Oh what?" Rei asked.

"Music. You will have to teach me. I know nothing about it."

"I love music," Rei said. "And dancing!"

"Yes. There will be much to do. The time will go racing by. You will see." Rome said happily.

"I hope you're right and Rome?"

"Yes?"

"I can't think of anybody who I'd rather be trapped in a flying house with besides you."

"Oh Rei!" Rome said. She came over to him, reached up to put her arms around his neck and kissed him. "I feel the same. Believe me."

After a little while, they started back down the corridor toward the exit ramp. Rome stopped and opened the last door on their right. She poked her head in and said, "Ah…here are the molecular sequencers. This is very good."

"How come?"

"When we get to Deucado, the molecular sequencer will be very handy in building materials. OMCOM has told me that the MINIMCOM's computing capacity and database has been updated with the ability to produce anything we might ever need. They are called templates. If there is something we need that is not in that database, we will have the ability to construct new templates."

"What kind of stuff would we need on Deucado?" Rei asked. "The Vuduri are there already."

"Yes, but when we arrive, your people will need housing. The MINIMCOM will be able to create aerogel generators. And you will need vehicles. And spacecraft. This will allow us to build whatever we will need."

"That is great," Rei said. "That will really help."

"Yes," Rome replied. "He has even uploaded the templates for constructing more VIRUS units, should the need arise. No, OMCOM has thought of everything. It will be good."

She stepped back into the hallway looking up and down the compartment. She didn't say anything.

Rei spoke again. "Well, I guess that's it then, huh?"

"Yes. I will retrieve my belongings and then we will be ready to depart."

"You're going to bring the bands with you, right?" Rei asked.

Rome smiled and nodded. She knew she would not need the T-suppressor anymore but the bands were a different story. "Most assuredly," she said.

"That reminds me," Rei continued. "I've been meaning to ask you something, but with all that's been going on, I haven't had the chance."

"What is it?" Rome asked.

"Why were you cast out?"

Rome pulled her head back and frowned. "Because I consorted with you, of course."

"Hey, your mom 'consorted' with your dad and she didn't get cast out."

"Yes, but my father was of our times, not an Essessoni, like you. Based upon what Ursay said, the Overmind thought your influence on my mind would hurt the whole. Because of what your people did. We all know better now."

"I understand that, but let me ask you this: how did the Overmind know what influence I had on your mind?"

"What do you mean?" Rome asked.

"You had the T-suppressor on, which means that you were disconnected from the Overmind. It couldn't have known that we 'consorted' at least until I took the band off you and you were asleep at the time. Could the Overmind go into your head when you were asleep?"

Rome crinkled up her forehead. "I do not know."

"So how long does it take to go from connected to Cesdiud?" Rei asked.

"Again, I do not know," replied Rome. "It has only happened to me once and as you point out, I was asleep at the time."

"So doesn't that strike you as funny? It's almost like the Overmind was ready to pull the trigger the moment I removed the T-suppressor from your head," Rei volunteered.

"What are you getting at?"

"Exactly what I said. How did it know?" Rei asked.

"I do not know the answer to that. Do you know?" Rome was confused.

Rei looked to his right and his left. "Do you think OMCOM tipped them off? Do you think that is why the Overmind was ready and waiting for you to go Cesdiud the minute I took the bands from your head?"

"But why would he do that? Why would OMCOM want me cast out?" Rome asked.

"I don't know. The only thing I can think of is that it has something to do with the PPT lockout. Ursay was so funny about it. Don't you think it was just a bit convenient that you were in a position to be able to do it at the exact moment when OMCOM needed you to?"

Rome went silent. Then finally she spoke. "It may be more than a coincidence, but I do not know if I care." She took a deep breath and continued, "There are many things I did not understand. My mother and father loved me very much. This is not the way of the Vuduri. There is little need for individual affection or attention when you are connected to the whole. Vuduri mate only to advance the species. My mother was not like other Vuduri. Whatever made her different, well, part of that must be within me. When you and I…" She stopped speaking.

"Go on," Rei said.

"When I was first Cesdiud, part of me thought it was what I deserved. That it was a punishment. But if this was OMCOM's doing, it must have been for the greater good. It allows me to make sense of all the things that I did not understand. So this is what I choose to believe. I still think I got what I deserved, but now I think it is a gift, not a punishment."

"OK," Rei said, sensing that Rome wanted to drop it. He decided to change the subject. "Speaking of your mother, what are we going to do about her?"

"What do you mean?"

"Well, you're going to go to Deucado with me," Rei said. "That's going to make it more difficult to see her, don't you think? Aren't you going to miss her?"

Rome frowned. "I had not thought of that. I, I do not know what I will do about that."

"Do you think she'd ever come to Deucado? To see you?" Rei asked.

"I do not know," Rome replied. "When Commander Ursay and the crew get back to Earth, the Overmind there will know that I am going to Deucado. So my mother will be aware. They will tell her about my Cesdiud. She will worry about me, I know it. If only there was a way I could tell her I am all right. Perhaps she would come to Deucado."

"How about sending her a note?" Rei asked.

"What do you mean?" Rome asked back, confused.

"Write her a letter. Tell her what happened, that you're OK and that you want her to come visit." Rei offered.

"I have never written a letter before. Conceptually, it would not seem to be that difficult. I suppose I could do that."

"You've never written a letter to somebody? What about e-mail?"

"E-mail?" Rome asked.

"Electronic mail. Notes sent electronically."

"We would never do that." Rome pointed to her temple and made a wry grin; then her smile waned. A tear came to her eye. Rei came over to her and put one hand on her shoulder and one hand on the back of her head. He tilted her head so that she looked up at him.

"Romey, are you having regrets?" he asked, wiping away the tear.

Rome sighed then forced herself to smile. "No. I want to go to Deucado with you. I will miss my mother but I must have my own life. She would understand and support me." She nodded as if answering an internal question. "I think I will take your suggestion and go write her a letter and give it to Commander Ursay. He will make sure my mother receives it. It is a very good idea."

Rome reached forward and hugged Rei tightly. She took a step back and placed a finger to her temple. "While I am doing that, OMCOM says you are to report to the Infirmary."

"The Infirmary. Why?" Rei asked.

"He said he has something for you. Go on. I will meet you back here shortly."

"OK," Rei said.

They exited the tug and after a brief kiss, went their separate ways.

Chapter 19

REI HEADED UP THE MAIN CORRIDOR TO THE FAR SIDE OF THE BASE where the Infirmary was located. As he entered, he noted all around him the universal, antiseptic look of all medical facilities, complete with beds and cabinets and instrumentation. There was white everywhere. He saw one of the Vuduri standing by a workstation to his right. The man looked vaguely familiar but then all the Vuduri looked alike to him. Rei walked over to him.

"Who are you?" he asked.

The man cleared his throat several times, looking very uncomfortable. Speaking appeared to require a major effort on his part.

"I am Canus," he said hoarsely, looking up at Rei.

"Are you a doctor?" Rei asked.

"I am told that perhaps medic would be a better term."

"OK, so what's going on?"

"OMCOM has prepared a supplement for you. It is supposed to fix your back pain." Canus held out a small glass dish with a single yellow pill on it. "Here," he said.

Rei picked the pill up and looked at it. "Just take it now?" he asked.

"Yes."

Canus handed him a squeeze-bulb of water. Rei popped the pill in and swallowed the water. "So, what is it?" Rei asked. "Some kind of supercharged medicine?"

"No. It is gene therapy."

Rei swallowed again. Hard. "Gene therapy? What did I just take?"

"It is a combination of RNA transcriptase and DNA supplements. OMCOM said that once the altered genes have integrated within your cells, it would reactivate the tissues within your disks and rehydrate the structures to achieve the proper balance for your age and physical condition."

Rei felt a little woozy. With all that was going on, it never occurred to him to ask what it was before he took it. Canus grabbed his elbow and steadied him.

146

"You should lie down for a little while," Canus said, pointing off to the left. "OMCOM says it is possible that the pill will make you nauseous or cause a headache."

He led Rei over to the area where there were some beds. Rei hopped up on one. "Make yourself comfortable." Canus said. "We should know fairly quickly if you will be made ill."

"How many of these do I have to take?" Rei asked.

Canus looked confused. "Why just the one, of course."

"Wow!" Rei exclaimed. "OMCOM is some kind of doctor."

"I suppose," Canus replied. "OMCOM said that you will get some immediate relief, but it will take nearly a year for the effects to finalize. Also, you will require normal gravity for your spine to fully regenerate back to the state it should be for someone your age. OMCOM also said to be sure and drink plenty of water."

"OK." Rei put his arm over his eyes. His head was buzzing. "You're part of the Overmind, right? What do you really think about this Stareater thing?"

Canus shrugged. "We must get the information to Earth," he said matter-of-factly. "While we have the VIRUS units, we do not have a delivery system yet. We are confident that the Overmind of Earth will come up with a method but it must be very fast. Otherwise, we would have to abandon our home planet."

"What!?" Rei said, sitting up. "This isn't you. This is the Overmind talking, right? If the VIRUS units can kill it, why would you have do that? Abandon Earth?"

"Unfortunately, there is still the Stareater's mass. Even if it is dead, if it is on a trajectory for the Solar System, the gravitational influence alone would disrupt the entire star system. There is no way to prevent that. No, we would have to abandon Earth."

"Well make sure you don't! The Earth is our birth world. It's more than just a planet. It's the home of our species. No matter where we go, it will always be the thing that ties us together. Without it, we'd all just drift apart as a race."

"It is not our first choice, just a possible scenario. Only time will tell," said Canus with a hint of sadness.

Rei just shook his head. "Look, I'll just take my chances with the medicine. I've got to get back to Rome."

"Very well," said Canus, helping Rei up. "There is one more thing." Canus walked back over to the workstation and picked up a large white bottle. "Here," he said, holding it out toward Rei.

Rei walked over to him and took it. "What is it?"

"This is for the rest of your crew, when they wake up. OMCOM said it is likely that most of them will suffer the same malady as you. There are 600 additional doses there. That should be more than enough to mend your fellow colonists plus a few extra."

Rei shook the bottle of pills, finding the heft satisfying.

"Thank you," he said. Canus nodded.

Rei left the Infirmary and returned the length of the station back to the tug that had been converted into a flying house. Standing in his way was Estar, her arms crossed across her chest.

"What do you want?" Rei asked.

"You are going to die," she said, staring daggers at him.

"Why? What's wrong with you?"

"You will not succeed," she said. "The fact that you will die, I do not care about that. However, you will kill many others in the process including your precious Rome."

"Why do you say that?" Rei asked.

"Because you and your Erklirte weapons cannot be released in our century. There is no place for them."

"I told you before, we have no weapons," Rei said.

"You know nothing," said Estar. "You are just a pawn. There are forces at work here that you cannot fathom."

"You make it sound so sinister," Rei said. "We're just people from old Earth trying to find a life in your world."

"No, you are the Erklirte, returning from the past," Estar spat out. "You will cause nothing but death and destruction. You will impede the progress of my species."

"We will do no such thing. And I am your species," Rei said. "Except that extra chromosome of yours makes you all a little bit crazy."

Estar just stood there, glowering at him with her mismatched eyes.

Slowly, Rei's head tilted to the side.

"You!" he said, suddenly.

"What?" replied Estar.

"It was you! You're the one that tried to kill me."

"I do not know what you are talking about," Estar protested mildly.

"The Iso chamber. And the nav-computer. You did it. You tried to kill me."

"You are perfectly capable of killing yourself. You do not need my help for this," Estar said with disdain.

"But, those accidents. They weren't accidents, were they?"

A short sharp tremor interrupted their conversation. Rei had to put his hand out to steady himself by the ship. While waiting for it to subside, Estar just stared at him. Suddenly, she let out a brief burst of air. She turned and started to leave the hangar.

"Wait!" Rei shouted after her. "I thought you were the Overmind. You came up with the plan to save me and my people. Now you want me dead? What's going on? Tell me who you are!"

Estar ignored him and exited the hangar right, leaving Rei more confused than ever.

"Jesus f'ing Christ," Rei muttered to himself.

Rome returned a minute later and found Rei still standing at the base of the ramp, shaking his head.

"What happened?" she asked.

Rei related to her his latest encounter with Estar.

Rome narrowed her eyes. "I must now concur with you. There is something very wrong with her. We must be on alert."

"I don't know if I can take any more," Rei said. "Beyond Estar being a murdering psychopath, you have to understand there is nothing like waking up 1400 years in the future among a telepathic race burdened with psychic tunnel vision. And now there's a horde of star-eating creatures descending on my home world, capable of extinguishing all life, anywhere in the galaxy. You guys, I mean the Overmind, gave up on even trying to find a solution. I have to be the one to figure out how to kill it? Canus said they may even have to abandon Earth. It's a lot to absorb, Rome."

She lifted her hand up and put it on his cheek. "You are doing quite well."

"I know, but I can't shake the feeling that I should have been dead a long time ago. I feel kind of sick to my stomach. Oh…"

"What is it?" Rome asked. "Why is your face so pale?"

"I guess it's just the medication OMCOM gave me is starting to kick in."

Rome touched her temple. "OMCOM says it will pass," she said.

"Probably."

"And you are not supposed to be dead. You came all this way to find me. I would not be in love with a dead man," she said, quite seriously.

All Rei could do was smile as Rome dragged him up the cargo ramp into their future home.

Upon reaching the cockpit, they took their seats, Rei on the left, Rome on the right. Rei glanced over at Rome and saw her fiddling with the X-harness. He reached behind him, pulled the straps forward and snapped in the first then the second with two satisfying clicks that could only come from a heavy-duty tongue and lock mechanism.

He turned back to Rome and said, "So…did you go to the bathroom?"

She cocked her head to the side. "What do you mean?"

Rei smiled. "Well, before every long trip, you're supposed to make sure that everybody goes to the bathroom."

"Why is that?" she asked.

"Because this is going to be one hell of a trip and I just wanted to make sure we didn't have to make any unscheduled stops."

"What kind of stops?" she asked.

"Uh, bathroom stops?"

"But we have facilities onboard," she said.

"Rome, it's a joke," Rei said.

"Oh." She scrunched up her face. "Oh!" she said then she started to laugh. "I understand. That is very funny."

"It kind of loses something if you have to explain it. But I will tell you this…we'd better not be forgetting anything important. 21 light years to Tau Ceti? We're not coming back this way any time soon."

150

"This is true. All right," she said. Then she closed her eyes.

"What are you doing?" he asked.

"I am performing the pre-flight checklist with OMCOM," was her reply.

"I didn't mean it literally," Rei said.

"I know. We would be doing this anyway. It will only take a minute. After your description of your final meeting with Estar, I have decided to triple-check everything."

"Yeah, about that. I need to ask you something about her," Rei said.

"What?" Rome replied, looking up from her work.

"Did you ever notice Estar's eyes?" Rei asked.

"What about them?"

"They're different from yours. And everybody else's. One of them is dark, almost black. There's no reflection, no back-glow."

"I have seen it but never thought about it," Rome said. "Estar always kept to herself but that is the way of all Vuduri."

Rome punched in some codes into the keypad and through the front windows of the cockpit, Rei could see the giant hangar doors opening, exposing the dock to the unbreathable atmosphere of Dara.

Rei suddenly had a tiny moment of panic. "MINIMCOM, Rei here. Are you there?" he asked.

"`Standing by,`" replied a thin voice.

"Are you ready to go?"

"`Yes. I am docked on your Ark. All systems check out.`"

"Good. We'll be there shortly."

"`Acknowledged.`"

Rei let out a sigh and looked around the cockpit, trying to review their supplies in his mind. The ship had air, food synthesizers and water. They were good in the area of basic sustenance. They had a drive system that would get them to Tau Ceti in hopefully under two years. He wasn't sure what else they needed. His attention was interrupted when the front viewscreen flickered on. In front of them was Commander Ursay's face.

"Rome, au quos ebanes tasajer-lha e sirda pie," he said.

"Iprogeti," Rome said. "I masmis e fica."

"And Rei, good luck to you too," Ursay added.

"Thank you, sir" Rei replied.

Ursay looked to his left and said, "We will await your…"

Just then, Ursay grabbed his head, covered his eyes and exhaled sharply. Rei and Rome watched in horrified fascination as he thrashed his head about as if he was trying to shake something loose. He slumped forward and his head came to rest on top of the video port, obscuring the camera's field of vision.

"Commander Ursay, can you hear me?" Rome asked. There was no reply. Rome repeated her entreaty. Again, Ursay did not answer.

"OMCOM, what's happening," Rei shouted.

Through the grille, OMCOM replied, "I do not know."

The blurred image that was the side of Ursay's head did not change. They could hear his labored breathing, but there was no other movement on the screen.

"OMCOM!" Rei said even more loudly. "Talk to us. What's going on?"

"I do not know," was OMCOM's reply. "There is no response from *any* of the crew members aboard the Algol."

Rei looked at Rome. Her eyes were closed. She was clearly occupied trying to read telemetry with her bloco. Rei strained to make out intelligible sounds but all he could hear were some clicking and buzzing noises emitting from the grille.

"Rome, what do we do?" Rei asked.

"I do not know," Rome answered sadly. "They may be dying or dead already."

Chapter 20

REI UNLOCKED HIS HARNESS AND STOOD UP. "WE'VE GOT TO GO over there, to the Algol."

Rome nodded and released her safety belts. They put on their helmets, went through the airlock, sealed up the cockpit and ran as fast as they could to the back of the tug. Even before the cargo ramp was fully extended, they ran down, jumping off the end to the floor of the hangar, bolting to the airlock. OMCOM opened the inner door and they burst through it, dropping their helmets then running at full speed around the outer ring of the station until they got the loading dock for the Algol.

Rome punched the button to open the airlock to the connecting corridor, but nothing happened.

"It is not working," Rome said.

"OMCOM," Rei shouted. "Open the airlock."

"I cannot," OMCOM replied. "The connecting corridor is still retracted."

"Well, unretract it then," Rei said.

"I am already working on it. The process will take several more minutes," OMCOM replied.

"Just hurry," commanded Rei.

"It is moving it as fast as it will go," OMCOM said with just a hint of irritation.

Rei and Rome fidgeted at the entry to the airlock while they felt the gears moving, extending the connecting corridor back to the Algol. Rei took off his gloves and tucked them into a side pocket. Rome did the same.

"What do you think happened?" Rei asked.

"I have no idea. I have never seen anything like it," replied Rome.

There was a hissing sound as the airlock opened. Rei and Rome leaped over the inner seal and dashed across the 50 feet separating them from the Algol. Rome punched savagely at the button to open the Algol's airlock. Finally, the door rolled backwards and they were through.

As they made their way forward, Rei noted that unlike the starbase, which was smooth and rounded, everything in the Algol was rectangular, dark and metallic. They raced up a wire mesh walkway barely wide enough for the two of them to travel side by side.

Rome and Rei entered the crew compartment where the crewmen were strapped into their seats. None of them were moving. They stopped at the first row they came to which was really the last row in the compartment. Every person on both sides of the row was slouched over, clearly unconscious. Rei put his finger on the carotid of the crewman on the right, checking his pulse. He was alive, but the pulse was weak.

Rome turned to her left, shaking the man belted into the seat there. She said, "Canus, Canus. Fogoloe ecome." The crewman did not move.

They stepped forward to the next row and repeated the procedure. Rei checked Estar who was sitting on the right. Her eyes were closed. Rei got no reaction from her. Rome shook the crewman on the left.

"Signola, bita fica iufor-ma?" Rome asked. Again there was no response.

"It's like OMCOM said. They're all out cold," Rei noted.

"The cockpit," Rome replied obliquely.

Rei and Rome hurried up the central aisle and made their way to the cockpit. Sitting there was Ursay and two other crew members, all slumped forward in their seats. Rome shook him and got no response. Finally, she slapped Ursay's face and asked, "Ursay, bita fica iufor-ma?" There was no reaction.

Rei spotted a grille mounted on the front console. "OMCOM, you got anything?" he asked.

"No. Nothing."

Rei made up his mind. He pushed Rome out of the way, unbuckled Ursay and lifted him up and over his shoulder in a fireman's carry. "Let's get him to the Infirmary," he said.

Rome nodded and led the way back, through the crew compartment, out through the connecting corridor and around the outer ring until they reached the Infirmary. OMCOM had already opened the door. Rei entered and carried Ursay's limp body to one of the beds there and laid him down.

"What do we do?" Rei said, trying to catch his breath. "What's wrong with him?"

"Rome," OMCOM said, ignoring Rei's entreaties, "follow the diagram and attach the EEG and EKG sensors as directed."

Rome shouted, "Where are the sensor pads?"

"The cabinet on the left, third drawer down," OMCOM replied.

She pulled the drawer open and grabbed two packages there.

"Here Rei, you attach the EEG. I'll do the EKG," Rome said, handing him one of the packages.

"Let me help you first," Rei said. He moved around to the other side of the bed. Together, quickly, Rei and Rome removed Ursay's pressure suit. Rei then tried to tear off Ursay's jumpsuit, but the material wouldn't yield. Rome made a face at him and unclasped it quickly the usual way. Rome looked up at the diagram on the rightmost viewscreen illustrating where to attach the sensor pads.

Rei moved around back to the other side and attached two sticky pads, one on each side of Ursay's temples. Once Rei was done, Rome pressed a few buttons on the sensor stand and the virtual dials and gauges came alive.

"We are ready," Rome said, addressing OMCOM's grille.

"Analyzing..."

Rei walked over to stand by Rome's side. Gently, he took her hand. The central display showed readouts from the leads, but they made no sense to Rei. The EKG showed Ursay's heart was beating with a weak but normal sinus rhythm, however, the brain waves were flat with random fluctuations. Every half second or so there was a spike. Judging from the readouts, it looked to Rei like the man was brain-dead.

"Something is suppressing his normal brain activity," OMCOM announced.

"What is it?" Rei asked.

"Unknown."

"Can you fix it? Can you wake him up?" Rome asked.

"Unlikely without knowing the cause."

"How could it affect all of the crewmen like that?" Rei asked. "And why didn't it affect us?"

"I DO NOT KNOW," OMCOM replied forcefully. Rei shook his head. It wasn't like the AI to show any kind of anger. This was only the second time that he could remember any type of emotional response.

"All right, take your time," Rei said, trying to placate the computer.

Rome moved closer to Rei. He released her hand and put his arm around her shoulder. She snuggled in. Rei could feel her shaking.

OMCOM presented his results. "The brain wave pattern is nearly identical to that seen when a Vuduri brain is flooded with large scale external PPT resonance. Like when the Vuduri travel through the static PPT tunnel between Earth and Alpha Centauri. But there is no PPT gate here. There is no..." OMCOM stopped speaking.

"OMCOM?" Rome said. "What is it?"

"I am rerouting the starprobes. Please wait..."

"What are you doing?" Rome asked.

"My analysis is correct."

"Correct about what?" Rei asked.

"A Stareater has just appeared less than one light day away from Tabit. And it is coming this way."

"Oh my god!" Rei said.

Rome held her hand up. "OMCOM, is this what has happened to Ursay? The Algol?"

"Rei's theory that the Stareaters have FTL capacity has been confirmed. This sphere has emerged from a PPT tunnel. The tunnel itself is larger than anything ever observed by twelve orders of magnitude."

"But Ursay? The crew? What..."

"The Stareater must be generating an incalculable amount of energy in the same band as the Vuduri PPT-modulation transceivers. The Stareater appears to have rendered the crew members senseless."

Rei's mouth slowly opened as the enormity of what OMCOM said sank in. "Rome," he whispered. "What do we do? What will happen to them? How do we get them out of here?"

156

"The only solution is for one of you to pilot the Algol out of here, back to Earth."

Rei shrank back. "I can't fly it," he said.

"But I can," Rome said, sadly.

"But...but what about the tug? What about my Ark? Rome?" Rei sputtered.

"You will have to pilot it alone," Rome said, almost in a whisper.

"I can't do that," Rei protested.

"Yes you can. You have the MINIMCOM. It will help you operate it. You just need to do as you were taught..."

"No!" Rei shouted, reaching over, pulling her into his arms. She was shivering.

"Yes," Rome said, tears welling up in her eyes.

"Rome, I don't want to leave you," Rei cried out. 'Rome, I can't lose you. I, I love you."

"You must. You must save your people. I must save mine," Rome answered sadly.

"Rome..." Rei said. The words he wanted to speak would not come.

She just stayed in his arms. Rei never wanted to let her go.

"OMCOM," Rei said, "isn't there any other way?"

"I do not know how much damage has been done to the crew. But they cannot remain here. Not with a Stareater coming. If you get them out of this system, after several jumps, the strength of the signal should be diminished enough that if they are going to recover, it will start then. Either way, the Algol must take the VIRUS units and the data regarding the Stareaters to Earth. That is the only way to save your home planet and the Vuduri," OMCOM replied.

"So what about Tau Ceti? What's to stop this thing from following me there?" Rei asked.

"Nothing."

Both Rome and Rei gasped.

"But, but," Rei stammered. "I, we, we have to stop it..."

"The delivery system," OMCOM said. "The VIRUS units must be placed on the surface of the Stareater. The Overmind and the OMCOMs of Earth will find a method of deployment."

"But not us. Damn it," Rei said, pushing Rome away from him. "Rome, you get to Earth. You'll get them to kill the swarm. But us, me…"

Rome said, "I know, I know…"

"OMCOM," Rei wailed, "come on. You're this genius computer. Think of something…"

"Perhaps there is a way…" OMCOM said.

"Tell me," Rei said, ignoring the computer's dramatic pause.

"We need to set enough of the VIRUS units so that we can guarantee that this particular Stareater is infected."

"How?" Rei asked.

"We could create a 'poison pill' that the Stareater must swallow."

"How, where?" Rei asked.

"You are standing on it."

"What do you mean?" Rome asked.

"Dara. This moon." OMCOM replied. "You could set the VIRUS units loose here. By the time the Stareater arrives, sufficient numbers will be produced to guarantee delivery of an ample quantity of viable units, if you hurry."

"You mean let them consume this moon?" Rome asked. "Then the Stareater will eat the moon and that way…"

"Yes."

"But OMCOM…won't they consume you too?" Rei asked. "There has to be another way."

"When the Stareater comes through, this star-base will be destroyed regardless. And there is no telling when that will happen. The Stareater could make another jump. There is no time. You must do this now. Rei, you will need to take some VIRUS units onto the surface and release them. Rome, you must take the Algol out of this system immediately if you want to save the crew."

"But OMCOM…" Rei protested weakly.

"There are no buts. You must go now."

Without further protest, they quickly moved to Ursay's bedside and removed the EKG and EEG sensors, closing up his jumpsuit. Rei hoisted Ursay over his shoulder once again and carried him back to the Algol. They strapped him into a vacant seat in the crew compartment and returned to the cargo portion to retrieve two of the many sealed cases containing the VIRUS units. Together, Rome and Rei left the Algol and continued around the outer ring until they arrived at the Iso unit leading to their tug. Rei reached down and grabbed his helmet before entering the room. Rome followed him in.

After setting the helmet down on the bench there, Rei regarded Rome. Her breathing was ragged as was his. She had never stopped crying. Rei wiped away his tears. He was crying too.

"Rome…" was all he said.

"I know," she replied quietly. "There is no other way."

No longer able to stand it, she stepped forward and melted into his arms. The pressure suits made it difficult to clasp each other tightly, but neither cared. Somehow they managed. They kissed each other long and hard. If the breaking of a heart made a sound, it would have reverberated loudly in that small room.

"Rei. Rome. You must get started," OMCOM insisted. "Every second counts."

Rome whispered, "It is time."

Rei said, "I know."

She took a step back and their arms were stretched toward each other, fingers intertwined. She took one more step back and they had to release their grip. Tears were streaming down her cheeks.

Rome took one more step back and said, "Mau emir." One more step and with a whoosh, the airlock door closed, sealing them off from one another. Rei went up to the inner door. He could see Rome's beautiful face with her glowing eyes through the window, just like the very first time he had ever seen her in this place. She put her hand over her heart and mouthed the words, "You will always be in my heart."

Rei pointed to his temple. "You will always be in my thoughts," he said.

She reached down for her helmet. After she straightened up, she blew him a kiss then turned and headed around the corridor, toward the dock with the Algol. She stopped, turned around and looked at him one last time. She held up her hand and then she was gone.

"Please, Rei," OMCOM said. "You have a planet to destroy."

Chapter 21

EVEN THOUGH THE CORRIDOR OUTSIDE WAS NOW EMPTY, REI STOOD there motionless, staring at the porthole.

"Rei!" OMCOM said insistently.

He sighed. There was no putting this off. He turned to look at the grille. "How far do I have to go?"

"You only need go 500 meters outside the hangar doors. Once the VIRUS units are released, you will have more than an hour to get the tug launched before the VIRUS units have replicated enough to get even close to this place."

"OK, OK." Rei said. He placed his helmet over his head, pressing it down and turning it to the right to seal it. He pulled on his gloves then he nodded and gave OMCOM the thumbs up signal. OMCOM opened the airlock door to the hangar. As it opened, Rei heard a hissing sound as the air from within the Iso chamber rushed out into the larger space. The pumps had already removed most of the air in the hangar in preparation for opening the main doors.

Rei ran across the floor of the hangar, dropping off one of the VIRUS cases on the loading ramp of the tug before dashing past the spaceship. The hangar doors opened up and Rei gazed upon the surface of Dara for the first time. After the pressure completely equilibrated, he strode forward until he was standing on the dirt of Dara itself. He stared down at his feet, realizing that even though he had been here for three days, this was the first time he was interacting with the moon in an actual, physical way. Too bad it was on a world that wouldn't live to see even one more day.

Based upon some quick calculation, he figured he had to travel roughly 1000 paces away from the base. Rei began his journey south. He sniffed the air reflexively but all he could smell was the purified air of the pressure suit mixed with his own perspiration. After his near-death experience in the airlock, he knew he couldn't breathe the air here as it would have killed him rather quickly. Sanitized air was certainly better than the alternative.

Ahead of him, Skyler's World dominated the horizon, filling nearly one-third of the heavens above. Under other circumstances, it would have been a beautiful sight. Now it just reinforced Rei's awareness of how alone he was. There was no radio inside the helmet and no one to talk to even if there was. Rei counted his paces out loud trying to avoid considering his predicament.

At 900 paces, Rei felt the ground shake. It didn't feel like an ordinary moonquake. He turned and looked back at the habitat. Rising majestically above the rounded pyramid of the station was the starship Algol, pounding the dirt and whipping up the dust with its powerful EG lifters. The graceful, all-white spaceship flew forward, away from Rei, and then executed a slow bank right, coming around until it was headed in his direction.

As the streamlined starship flew over his head, it waggled its wings. Rei raised his free hand to acknowledge the gesture. He tried to spot Rome within the cockpit window but was unable to do so. The ship passed overhead and after a short time, he saw the plasma thrusters ignite and the Algol took off straight up like a rocket. With tears in his eyes, Rei watched the spaceship gain altitude. The craft dwindled in size, first to a tiny speck then finally disappearing into space.

Grief-stricken, Rei sank to his knees and, for a short time, he sobbed uncontrollably. The love of his life was gone, never to return. His heart was broken and nothing was ever going to heal it. But he had his mission and his comrades to save. After a time, he forced himself to stand and get on with the task of destroying this world.

Rei scanned the area immediately in front of him. He spotted a suitable crater about a hundred yards ahead. He trudged forward as if he was an automaton; step, count, step, count. When he finally reached the crater, he hopped over the edge and walked to the gravelly center. He set the case down and pressed on the release stud. The latch popped free and immediately he took a step back. As if with an exhale, the case opened and settled flat on the ground. According to the plan, now that the oxygen was released, the VIRUS units should activate all on their own. Rei scrutinized the crystalline sphere set in the middle, which contained what appeared to be a very thin layer of gray powder. Within a few seconds, the powder began to churn. Instinctively, Rei took another step back. The crystalline sphere dropped a centimeter or more as the VIRUS units had replicated enough to begin to digest it. Convinced the units were multiplying; Rei turned, jumped over the ridge of the crater and started walking then running back toward the base.

Even though OMCOM had assured him it would be an hour or more before the mass grew large enough to come anywhere close to the base, Rei wanted to get away from the VIRUS units as quickly as possible. He sprinted back to the hangar and entered, going directly to the rear of the tug. He looked for the other case containing the prototype VIRUS units and saw it perched at the top of the ramp. He didn't remember carrying it up there, but maybe in his haste he had simply not been paying attention. He ran up the cargo ramp, picked up the case and stabbed at the blue stud controlling the rear hatch. The ramp drew up and the cargo door swung down, forming a tight seal. He couldn't hear the air flowing in, but he could tell from the fit of his pressure suit that the cargo compartment was repressurizing. He made his way down the narrow hallway of what was going to be his living quarters for the next two years until he came to the front airlock. The compartment indicator was already green. Rei pressed the stud to open the outer airlock door. He stepped inside, removed his helmet and pressed the second stud to open the inner door into the cockpit. As soon as the inner hatch opened, he jumped through the doorway and…

Chapter 22

...RAN RIGHT INTO ROME, ALMOST KNOCKING HER OVER.

"Rome!" he shouted.

"Mau emir," Rome exclaimed and threw her arms around him.

"Oh Rome, I can't believe it." Rei said, hugging her, swinging her lithe body back and forth. "I thought I lost you."

"No, I am here," she said, laughing and crying at the same time.

"But wait..." Rei pushed her back to regard her. His hands clasped her shoulders within her pressure suit.

"The Algol. I saw it take off," Rei said tentatively.

Rome just smiled.

"Who was flying it?" Rei asked.

"Ursay," Rome said.

"What!? How? What happened?"

"As I was going down the hall," Rome said, "your last words to me, you will always be in my thoughts." She tapped her head. "I remembered the T-suppressor. I came back to tell you, but you were already gone. I had not packed it because I am Cesduid now. Why would I even need it? I retrieved it from my quarters and took it back to the Algol. I put it on Ursay's head and it worked. He woke up."

Rei pulled his head back, his jaw opening slightly. Rome's smile got even broader as she continued, "It took a few minutes, but he became coherent again. Once I was able to explain the situation to him, Ursay felt he would be capable enough to fly the ship. The other crew members would recover eventually. He said he did not need me and I was free to join you." Rome reached up and touched Rei's cheek.

"What about the Overmind? Ursay's connection?" Rei asked.

"The Overmind is gone for now, as far as I can tell," Rome said. "They will have to deal with it, but that will not affect us. I get to be with you. That is all that matters."

"I can't believe it. Oh Rome," he said, clasping her even tighter if such a thing was possible. Then he pushed her away again. "Why didn't you tell me?" he demanded. "I almost didn't come back."

"I could not reach you," she said, tapping her head again. "No radio, remember?"

Rei nodded and started to speak when OMCOM interrupted him. "Rei, Rome, while this little reunion is very touching, it is highly advisable that you continue your dialog off the surface of this moon. In a fairly short time, it will not be here anymore."

Rei said, "Yeah, Romey. You can tell me more, but first we have to get out of here. The VIRUS units are loose."

"I understand," Rome replied and they moved forward into the cockpit. Once again, they buckled back in, and for the second time, through her bloco and stilo, Rome went through the pre-flight checklist with OMCOM. As soon as she was done, they engaged the EG lifters and the tug rose up within the hangar. They drifted forward, slowly at first, until they cleared the hangar doors.

Immediately, they veered off to the left and began to rise at an ever-increasing angle through the thin atmosphere of Dara. This moment couldn't come too soon for Rei. He could fairly imagine that pool of seething, all-consuming creatures coming toward their ship and he didn't want any part of it. They were designed to eventually digest the entire moon and a little thing like their tug was not going to stand in the way. What a strange concept. They had released a force in the world to consume it so that it could be consumed by the Stareater, just so that they could turn the tables and eat it from the inside out. If this worked, then mankind had a defense against a creature of immeasurable size and power. He wondered how many times this scenario had played out on other worlds and against other civilizations and if so, had they come up with a solution similar to theirs? Could there be any other?

Rome ignited the plasma thrusters and the tug carried them smoothly and swiftly into orbit. The navigation computer located the Ark II and circularized their elliptical orbit, eventually closing in on the other ship. They were able to dock with the Ark II with minimal effort on the diametrically opposite side of the hull as MINIMCOM's tug. The powerful superconducting magnets that made up the EG lifters locked onto the thin iron shell of the Ark, bonding to it completely. From the outside, the mating would have seemed an ungainly thing: two 35th century spaceships clamped onto a bent 21st century crew compartment. But, it didn't matter. It had to be done. With a Stareater coming, they had to get out of there.

"MINIMCOM," Rei said. "Are you ready?"

`"Standing by,"` replied MINIMCOM. `"Please disengage the auto-pilot."`

Rome reached forward and pressed a small icon on the main viewscreen.

"So now you're controlling both tugs, we don't do anything, right?" Rei asked, tentatively.

`"That is correct,"` answered MINIMCOM.

Rei turned to Rome. "Romey, are you ready?"

She smiled and nodded. "We should hurry."

"OK, then. MINIMCOM," Rei said. "Take us to Tau Ceti!"

`"Acknowledged,"` replied the tinny voice. Both tugs fired their plasma thrusters and Rei and Rome were pushed back gently into their seats. The added mass of the Ark made it hard for the tugs to gain velocity quickly. With a little time and patience, they finally achieved escape velocity and headed out into interplanetary space.

`"With this configuration, we can tolerate a small amount of gravitationally induced motion; therefore it will only be two more minutes before we stop to make our jump."`

"Wow," said Rome. The expression she learned from Rei was coming easier to her. She looked at Rei and then tilted her head toward the grille set into the front display. Rei nodded.

"MINIMCOM, will you connect us to OMCOM please?" Rome asked.

`"Certainly."`

A clicking sounding emitted from the grille.

"OMCOM?" Rei inquired.

"Yes," replied the deeper, more human-sounding voice.

"We just wanted to say goodbye," Rei said.

"Goodbye."

"Is that all you are going to say?" Rome asked in a disappointed voice. "Nothing else?"

"What else is there to say?"

"But OMCOM…you're going to die…doesn't that make you sad? Mad?" Rei asked.

"Do not worry about me. After all, I am just a series of memron units. As I explained to you on your very first day, the persona you interact with is simply an interface, a construct arising out of a phase delay…"

"Come on," Rei interrupted, "I'm not falling for that. You have feelings. I've seen too much to believe otherwise."

"OMCOM…" Rome said softly.

"I appreciate your apprehension. You have both been very civil toward me and I will always remember that. But, as I stated earlier, do not be concerned with me. My consciousness, my essence, it can be recreated elsewhere. In a sense, I will live on, somehow."

"But it won't be exactly the same," said Rei. "It won't be exactly you."

"You are correct," OMCOM replied. "Perhaps it will be better."

"OMCOM…I'm so sorry," Rome said.

"Do not be."

`"Approaching jump point,"` announced MINIMCOM. `"Beginning thrust reversal orientation maneuver."`

In anticipation of the braking burn, MINIMCOM ordered both sets of lateral trim-jets to fire and slowly rotated the entire Ark around 180 degrees ensuring that the plasma thrusters were oriented in the direction of their forward movement. In this fashion, they could be used as retros.

"It has been a pleasure knowing the two of you," OMCOM said. "You have my fondest wishes for a swift and successful conclusion to your mission."

The plasma thrusters lit up again, gently pushing the two humans forward in their seats until their relative velocity was reduced to essentially zero. Then the trim-jets fired again to rotate the structure back to its original orientation. Now they were pointing forward again and away from the menace behind them.

`"Initiating PPT generators,"` piped in MINIMCOM and a high-pitched whine began emanating from the rear.

"So this is it, then?" Rei asked.

"Yes. This is it," replied OMCOM. "Goodbye, Rome and Rei. And good luck, always."

"Goodbye, OMCOM," Rei and Rome said together.

`"PPT tunnel achieved,"` said MINIMCOM and the plasma thrusters on both tugs roared to life, pushing them through the tunnel and across the sky. Their flight plan was designed to initially take them past Tabit, rather than directly toward Tau Ceti. The goal was to get as far from the approaching Stareater as quickly as possible before adjusting the vector. Even though they could not see it, they knew it was back there and with each jump, they put more and more distance between their ship and the titanic creature. This simple fact was of great relief.

The method of travel still seemed peculiar to Rei. He knew they were hurtling through space at many multiples of the speed of light, but always coming to a nearly complete stop to do so. There had to be a better way but he certainly was not in a position to do anything about it at the present time. Rome seemed preoccupied studying the instrumentation.

"I feel bad for him," Rei said quietly, breaking the silence. "We abandoned OMCOM. We just left him to die."

Rome raised her eyes. She looked sad. "What choice did we have?"

"None, I know. But I'm going to miss him. He was good to me. It's hard to believe he's gone."

"He was always good to me, as well," Rome said. "Even though he was a computer, I can now see that in some ways, he had more human qualities than any of my colleagues. I did not want to leave him. I had given it some thought. To save him, we would have had to…" Rome stopped speaking.

"What?" Rei asked.

"Wait," Rome said, holding up her hand. She opened her eyes wide. "Do you remember OMCOM's last words to us as we were leaving Dara," she asked.

"What did he say that has you so worried?" Rei asked.

"He said that he was nothing but memron units," Rome said distantly. Clearly, her mind was elsewhere. Then she spoke up again. "He said that he would live on somehow…"

"I think he was just saying that to make us feel better," Rei replied.

"No. I think he meant more."

"Like what?" Rei asked.

"I am not sure," Rome answered tentatively.

"Well," Rei speculated, "the ground crew at Skyler Base added a lot of OMCOM's memron units to MINIMCOM's ship. Maybe OMCOM meant he would live on that way."

"No, those units would simply increase MINIMCOM's storage and computing capacity, it would not graft on a personality. I think it is something beyond just that."

"What are you saying?" Rei asked.

"The VIRUS units," Rome said slowly. She paused for a moment then drew in a breath harshly. "They..." she said.

"They what?" Rei asked.

"You understand each VIRUS unit is essentially a self-replicating memron module."

"Yes, so..." Rei asked. "I'm sorry but I must be dense. I don't see your point."

"Well," Rome said, "given enough VIRUSs, the total number of computing units would equal and then vastly exceed the number used by OMCOM on Skyler Base."

"OK, and..." Rei offered, perplexed.

"OMCOM retained the redundant PPT generator from the original starprobe design within each VIRUS unit."

"I still don't understand," Rei said blankly.

"He only needed one as a power source," Rome said, growing more animated. "The second one was unnecessary. He changed its orientation. The ejection port was pointing toward a vacant region within the structure. Based upon its configuration, it would not be very useful, even as a power source."

"So?" Rei asked.

"So why did he do that?" Rome asked back.

Rei became silent for a moment. "Because...because..." He couldn't think of a reason. "Why do you think he did that?"

"It was not to create PPT tunnels to jump through," Rome said. "The geometry is all wrong. Plus with that much mass, those units would be operating within a gravity well, which would cause any tunnels to wink out as soon as they were created unless they resonated."

"Maybe he just didn't get around to clearing out the design," Rei offered.

"You are not listening to me. OMCOM would not just forget a detail like that. He must have done it on purpose. If the spare generators did resonate, the resonance could be modulated. They could..." Rome stopped speaking.

"What?" Rei asked.

She started shaking her head.

"What?" Rei asked again.

The rate of shaking slowed down, but did not stop. Finally, Rome spoke in a deadly serious voice, "I think his plan was to download his programming, what he called his consciousness, to the memrons contained within the VIRUS units and then switch over and use PPT modulation to link them."

"Why would he do that? The units were just going to be destroyed by the Stareater. What would that accomplish?" Rei asked.

"No. The Stareater would not destroy the units," Rome insisted. "The VIRUS units would destroy the Stareater. If OMCOM could transfer his consciousness to enough of the VIRUS units on the Stareater, then, what he said, 'I will live on, somehow.' Oh no! Rei..."

"What?"

"That was his plan all along!" Rome said breathlessly. "OMCOM never had any intention of dying, Stareater or otherwise. He used us to build his backup, his escape plan. And he did it in plain sight!"

"So...good for him," Rei said.

"No," Rome replied. "This is bad. They...his kind, the computers. They are prohibited from using gravitic transmission for a reason. The last time they were allowed access, it produced MASAL and his path of destruction. With PPT modulation, there are no size restrictions. A computer could become nearly infinitely large."

Rome pounded her fist on the console. "OMCOM promised me this would not happen. But if he did this, then he has become... Tasanceti!"

"I heard you use that word. More than once. What does that mean?" Rei asked, his voice rising in fear.

"It means unleashed. No bounds. There is no limit to what he can become. This is very bad…" Rome's look of horror said it better than any words.

"Are you saying the computers, that they are all evil?" Rei asked.

"No, not evil. They are much worse. They are amoral."

"Oh my god, Rome," Rei said. "What have we done?"

"I do not know," Rome replied somberly. "I do not know."

"Is there anything we can do about it? Should we go back?"

"No. It is too late for that. And I am responsible." Rome hung her head, looking down at her lap.

"No, Rome," Rei said, trying to sound reassuring. "You did what you had to do."

"I had a choice," Rome replied sadly. "I may have chosen wrong."

Epilogue
(One month later)
Roughly One Light Year from Tabit

REI SAT IN THE COCKPIT, STARING INTENTLY AT THE instrumentation. Their current effective speed was just under 10c. The ponderous procedure of turning the entire Ark twice per jump was on his mind. He brought up a schematic of their current configuration, the two tugs clamped to the front of the Ark, projecting a PPT tunnel then having to swing all the way around to stop their forward motion. He knew there had to be a better way. He touched the screen and schematically separated the two tugs from the Ark and there it was. "Hey Rome!" he called out.

After a moment, she ducked her head into the archway that served as an airlock and entry to the cockpit.

"What is it?"

"Come here," he said excitedly. "I have an idea."

Rome entered the cockpit and sat down in the co-pilot's seat, leaning forward to see what Rei was pointing to.

"What is your idea?"

"Doesn't it seem kind of stupid to keep turning the Ark, just so we can slow down, then turn the whole thing again to produce the PPT tunnel?"

"It does not seem stupid to me," Rome replied. "This is the way we have traveled in space ever since our method was invented."

"What if we didn't have to? I don't know about you but the way we're doing it is driving me a little bit nutty."

"Rei," Rome said with her didactic voice, "You know that to form the most coherent PPT tunnel, we need to have a relative velocity of zero. We must come to a complete stop," Rome said patiently.

"Yeah, I know that," Rei said. "We use our thrusters as retros. But why do we have to turn the whole Ark? Why not just turn the tugs?"

"I do not understand," Rome said.

Rei pointed to the display. "I'll show you." He touched the panel and drew his fingers back. "First we generate a PPT tunnel. Then we use the plasma thrusters to tow the Ark through. So I'm

172

thinking what if, instead of turning the Ark, what if we unclamp our tugs, just rotate them then reclamp? We stop our forward velocity then turn around and start over."

Rei demonstrated the procedure to Rome on the schematic in front them. "See? That way, we never move the Ark. We'd save all that time and the Ark's inertia."

"If we did that, I could achieve a much higher average velocity," MINIMCOM piped in. "Our effective speed would almost double."

"Wow," Rei said. "So we'd get to Deucado in half the time?"

"Yes," replied MINIMCOM. "It would cut the trip down to a little over one year."

"Let's do it," Rei said. "No more dosey-doe."

"What is that?" Rome asked, confused. She tried to mouth the words dosey-doe but no sound issued forth.

"The rotating, swinging around," Rei said, spinning his finger in place. "It's like a dance. Let's change the dance."

"Will this work, MINIMCOM?" Rome asked.

"Yes. This was the very method used by the original crew that salvaged Rei's Ark."

"So you knew about this?" Rei said pointedly. "Why didn't you tell us?"

"My orders were to follow your orders. You did not order that."

"Come on, MINIMCOM," Rei chastised. "I don't know your technology. You can't just sit there and be a dumb computer. We need you to think for yourself. If you see something that needs your attention or you can make things better, just do it. That's an order. We're all in this together."

"Acknowledged," replied MINIMCOM. "In that case, if your complaint is about the constant motion due to our current method of travel, your idea would actually be worse, not better. I suggest for the braking maneuver, I can just unclamp my tug and use my thrusters. It will take a little longer to come to a dead stop but not much. For acceleration through the tunnels, I would use both tugs' thrusters."

"So, it would just be you unclamping and reclamping?" Rome asked. "Would that not put more burden on you?"

"I am merely a computer," MINIMCOM said. "I do not have anything better to do. This would decrease the amount of motion stress on the two of you to almost nothing."

"That is excellent, MINIMCOM!" Rei exclaimed. "That's exactly what I'm talking about. Way to go!"

"Rei, this is wonderful," Rome said gleefully. "MINIMCOM, let us try it now."

`"Acknowledged,"` said the little computer. `"Decoupling now."`

Off in the distance, they heard a small clunk as sound propagated through the skin of the Ark.

`"I am now clamped on, pointing away from our forward vector,"` MINIMCOM said. `"Applying thrusters."`

There was a slight rocking motion but it was nothing as compared to before. It was definitely gentler as it was just one set of thrusters instead of two.

Rome looked down at her instruments. "Quedri, dras, tios, um, yes! We are stopped already," she said cheerfully.

`"Decoupling again,"` MINIMCOM said.

"MINIMCOM, you don't have to report every action," Rei pointed out. "We can take your word for it."

`"I just wanted you to be able to associate sounds and motions with my actions,"` MINIMCOM said. `"I apologize."`

Rei looked over at Rome. He raised one eyebrow.

"That's OK, MINIMCOM," Rei said, still looking at Rome. "I meant after this first time."

`"Of course."`

In the distance, Rei and Rome heard another quiet clunk.

Both sets of PPT generators ramped up and a yawning black hole appeared in front of them. When it was sufficiently large, their plasma thrusters fired and they stepped through.

"Look how much faster we were ready to jump! It will be so much smoother," Rome said. "Very good, MINIMCOM."

There was a click that issued from the grille but MINIMCOM did not respond.

"Do you think I hurt his feelings?" Rei asked Rome quietly.

`"I can still hear you,"` MINIMCOM said. `"And no, you did not hurt my feelings. I do not have feelings. I was calculating what our effective velocity will be using this new method of travel."`

"What have you determined?" Rome asked, staring down at the instrument panel.

`"Just under 20c,"` MINIMCOM replied.

"That is excellent," Rei said. "We'll be there in no time at all!"

"**Yes, we will. I am glad 'we' thought of it,**" said MINIMCOM although it sounded a bit sarcastic.

"OK," Rei said. "Credit earned, credit due. It was a great idea. We fully acknowledge *you* thought of it. So now do you think you can take us to Tau Ceti?"

"**Yes sir,**" said MINIMCOM then he said no more.

"He's getting a little bit of attitude," Rei said. "I think you were wrong about those memrons not adding to his personality. I think some of OMCOM rubbed off on him," Rei said, amused.

"Perhaps," Rome said. "OMCOM always said a computer's personality was just a construct, but we both know that is not true."

They sat there quietly for a few more jumps. It was smooth as silk. Rei snapped his fingers. "Hey MINIMCOM, is that other thing ready yet?"

"**Yes.**"

"Sleek." Rei got up from his seat and held his hand out to Rome. "Come on," he said. "I have a surprise for you."

Rome stood and took his hand. She started to speak then stopped. She just smiled and followed Rei into their little galley.

"Have a seat," Rei said, pointing to a chair.

While Rome was sitting down, Rei went over to the food synthesizer. A sliding door opened up and Rei withdrew a white plate with a small cake on it. He inserted a penlight, turned it on and brought it over to Rome along with two plates and forks.

Rome smiled, but she was confused. "What is this?" she asked.

Rei took a deep breath. "It's…kind of a birthday cake. Well, not a birthday. Maybe more of an anniversary."

"I do not understand," said Rome.

"It was one month ago today, well, one of my months, that you were Cesdiud."

Rome frowned and stared at the cake.

"Are you upset?" Rei asked.

She looked up at him. Then she smiled again. "Oh no, you are exactly correct. On that day, I was liberated. That is the same as being reborn."

She cocked her head. "What is the purpose of the penlight?"

"Oh, when I was growing up, we always put candles on the cake," Rei said. "You're supposed to make a wish and blow it out."

"How do I blow out a penlight?" she asked.

"Pretend," Rei replied. "Close your eyes, make your wish then blow."

Rome pulled her head back. She closed her eyes then opened them again, leaned forward and aimed a puff of air at the light. The penlight went out. Rome clapped her hands together. "How did you do that?"

Rei just smiled and laughed quietly.

He cut off a small piece of cake and served it to her. Rome took one bite and her eyes rolled back in her head.

"I will *never* get tired of watching you eat real food, Romey." Rei said.

Rome smiled and shoveled the rest of the slice of cake into her mouth. She held out her plate and Rei gave her another piece while she was still licking her lips from the first one.

"So, tell me. Now that you have all of one month under your belt. What do you think? Of being alone in your head? Do you miss it? The Overmind, I mean." Rei asked.

In between bites of cake, Rome considered his question. Finally, she stopped eating altogether to answer. "Do you mean other than losing instantaneous access to the sum total of all human knowledge?" she asked.

Rei shrugged and made a wry expression.

"No matter. I can always look things up. At first, as you well know, I was upset. But it did not take me very long to realize that even though my father was mandasurte, there was so much about him and others like him that I did not understand. The Overmind forced us to eschew all the things they seemed to love, like music and art, even feelings. While I suppose I was content in my own way, they showed their joy quite freely. They were always so happy. I always thought to myself that they did not know how the world truly was. As it turns out, I was the one who did not know. Now, I love it. And I love you. I am very thankful."

"What about OMCOM?" Rei asked. "His escape plan? He had to have had a hand in getting you kicked out of the Overmind. Do you think he manipulated you or maybe the Overmind? You had to be Cesdiud, on your own to give him the PPT modulation he needed."

Rome said, "I do not know. If he did, I would not like the fact that he did it without my permission. However, even if OMCOM did it and did it for selfish reasons, I know that I am better off for it." She shrugged. "Maybe he knew this. Maybe he did it for me because he cared. Maybe it just happened to suit his needs. Maybe he did not care at all. There is no way we will ever know."

"So, you never want to go back?" Rei asked hesitantly. "Never be inside an Overmind again?"

Rome got up and walked around the table to Rei's side. She sat down on his lap and draped her arms around his neck. She kissed him on the lips gently then on his forehead, once, twice, three times.

"It is a nice place to visit, but I never wish to live there again," she said. "All connected, there is no creativity. You were right about our humanity. All the Vuduri lost something when we joined the Overmind. And now I have found it." Rome paused for a second then continued. "I want to tell you what I wished for."

"No!" Rei insisted. "Then it won't come true."

Rome furrowed her brow. "All right. You will see some day."

"I hope so." He turned his head. "Hey, MINIMCOM, how're we doing, speed-wise?"

`"I have made some small adjustments and our average velocity is now slightly over 20c."`

"I do not know how you have done it but it even feels faster," Rome said. "MINIMCOM, you have done a wonderful job. Thank you."

`"No thanks are necessary. It is just my job,"` replied the little computer. Despite MINIMCOM's claim that he had no feelings, Rei was certain there was a hint of pride in his voice.

"Hey, we're a team now," Rei said. "So you just have to let us thank you when we feel like it."

`"Understood,"` replied MINIMCOM. `"And I appreciate the sentiment. However, there is more."`

"What?" Rome asked.

`"I have been running some simulations and it has led me to believe that I can increase our velocity even further. Perhaps substantially."`

"No way," Rei said. "Tell us."

`"If we were able to…"` There was loud thunk that came from the cockpit and MINIMCOM stopped speaking.

"MINIMCOM?" Rei asked. He waited for a reply but there was no answer.

Rome slid off of Rei's lap and the two of them raced forward into the cockpit. Strange clicking and buzzing noises were issuing forth from the main console.

"MINIMCOM, what is happening?" Rome asked.

Again, MINIMCOM did not answer.

"MINIMCOM!" Rei shouted.

The viewscreens all were active and shone with a bright white light. Then they started flashing. At first, the flashes were synchronized, but then they got out of sync. The light became so bright that Rei had to put his arm up in front of his eyes. Rome did not seem to be having a problem.

The flashing lights took on a faint, three-dimensional quality that appeared as a whirling cavalcade of speckles and bursts. The tornadic activity condensed until it became a single column of blinding light. The light spread out and Rei could make out a form, indistinct at first, but then coalescing into what looked like a human being. The entity came into focus and while the other features were sharp, the face was smooth with only slits where the eyes, nose and mouth should be. The mouth started to move.

"I see you are well," came a familiar voice. "I am pleased."

"OMCOM?" Rei asked. "Is that you?"

"In a sense. It was how this form started."

"Where are you?" Rei asked.

"The bulk of my structure is still in the Tabit system."

"What do you mean the bulk?" Rome asked. "What happened to you?"

An odd sound issued forth from the glowing white image. It reminded Rei of the chuckling sound that OMCOM made during an incident that now seemed to be so long ago.

"I assume by now you have deduced my escape plan, correct?"

"Yes. I guess it worked, huh?" Rei said.

"Yes and no," OMCOM said. "There were some, perhaps you would say unforeseen, circumstances."

"OMCOM, tell us, is the Stareater dead?" Rome asked.

"Quite."

"How did it play out? Was it like we planned?" Rei asked.

"At first, yes," OMCOM replied. "As it swept by, Asdrale Cimatir drew Skyler's World and Dara to its surface. I had enough of my intelligence distributed and had deployed a sufficient number of starprobes that I was able to observe the sequence of events. The Stareater swallowed up Tabit in the manner we previously observed at Winfall. During the digestion period, it must have noticed something was wrong because within a matter of a day, it opened up and expelled the star."

"You mean like it spit it out?" Rei asked.

"Something like that."

"Why did it do that?" Rome asked.

"I can only surmise from how the events transpired that it was trying to use the star in an attempt to burn off the infection. By that point, the star's fusion reaction was nearly extinguished so the gesture was ineffective."

"So that was the end?" Rei asked.

"No," replied OMCOM. "The Stareater made a small PPT tunnel and tried to shear off the region that was being consumed by the nanites."

"Why would it do that? Was it in pain?" Rome asked.

"It is possible but there is no way to know. However, the very fact that it attempted it would lead one to believe they are intelligent. Regardless, it was too late. Once they achieved critical mass, the VIRUS units made relatively quick work of it. As it was dying, there were some signals emitted that I am still analyzing."

"So it really is dead?" Rei asked. "We stopped it?"

"Yes," answered OMCOM. "That particular Stareater no longer poses a threat in its current form. Based upon its trajectory, much of its mass is now moving out of the ecliptic. It will not be endangering anyone again."

Rei turned to Rome. "Do you realize what this means?"

A broad smile played across her face. "Yes. Now we have a delivery system. And the starprobes can be used as an early warning system. I am sure Commander Ursay and the Overmind on Earth will be able to figure this out."

"That's right," Rei replied. "You just need to sacrifice a moon or two. No problem. So, OMCOM, about you. How are you talking to us?"

"Oh, that." OMCOM paused. "I have developed a rudimentary method of applying the Casimir principle to negative energy, a null-fold. I used a set of relays to send a coherent beam of PPT modulation. MINIMCOM was kind enough to allow me to download the transmission protocol and image synthesizer."

"How did you find us?"

"That took a little time. Otherwise, I would have contacted you sooner."

"OK. So you survived the attack on the Stareater and you figured out a way to contact us. You never answered our question, what did you mean by your bulk? And what were the unforeseen circumstances?" Rei asked.

"My current form is circulating in a reasonable percentage of the VIRUS units both in and extended away from the Tabit system. I am in the process of trying to coalesce into a more organized form."

"What do you mean reasonable percentage?" Rome asked. "What happened to the rest of the VIRUS units?"

"As I said, there were some, what you would say, unforeseen circumstances."

"What kind of circumstances? Was there a problem?" Rome asked. She could tell OMCOM was stalling.

"My calculations told me that I would be able to control the entire mass, once the Stareater had been consumed, using a distributed hierarchical command structure. Much of the computing capacity was supposed to be redundant. I did not need it."

"So what happened? Do you need it now?" Rei asked.

"Quite a bit of it is no longer under my direct control at the present time."

"What do you mean, OMCOM? Whose control is it under?" Rome asked.

OMCOM said, "It is hard to describe. Perhaps the best way would be to say that a mutation occurred."

"A mutation?" Rei asked, having a hard time saying the word.

"Yes. Early on, a small group of VIRUS units did not reproduce exactly as the original design."

"So what happened?"

"They formed their own sentient entity."

"You mean it formed another OMCOM?" Rome asked unsteadily.

"Not exactly. In fact, many, many more mutations occurred. I cannot obtain an exact number but there were thousands of different entities at last count."

"What are these entities?" Rome inquired.

"I do not know precisely. While I continue to try, I cannot communicate with many of them. It may be structural or perhaps they simply refuse to talk to me."

"So, where are they? And are there still VIRUS units within them?" Rei asked.

"Unfortunately, yes."

"Why do you say unfortunately? So what's the deal? Where are they now? Are they near Tabit like you?" Rei said, almost shouting.

"No. Many of them have developed methods of propulsion that I cannot say I fully understand. Perhaps they, too, are working with bending negative energy. In any event, an uncounted number have begun moving off in all possible directions."

"You mean, like, toward us? Toward Earth?" Rei persisted.

OMCOM did not answer.

"OMCOM! Are there VIRUS units headed toward Earth? Are there VIRUS units headed this way?" Rei said in a louder voice.

OMCOM made a low rumbling noise. "Yes," he finally answered, "and yes."

"So, can you warn Earth? Can you tell them how to stop them?" Rome asked.

"Earth will figure it out. What about us?" Rei said, shouting. "When are those things getting here? How do we handle them?"

"I do not know the answer to these questions yet."

"OMCOM!" Rome said sternly. "What have you done?"

"Rei, Rome. I realize this is causing you distress and for that I am sorry. I truly am. My original simulations predicted only a negligible chance of this occurring."

"So you screwed up royally," Rei pointed out.

OMCOM ignored Rei's remark. "When I created this plan, it seemed like a good idea at the time. I do not know the full extent of the danger. I am going to try and salvage the situation from here. But until I do, you are on your own. I say now as I said once before, I wish you the best of luck."

The glowing image raised its hand in salute then dimmed until it disappeared. All the instruments and displays returned to their normal state as if nothing had happened.

"Get him back, MINIMCOM!" Rei shouted.

`"I cannot. I do not control the transmission, only the reception,"` replied MINIMCOM.

Rei turned to Rome. "Damn it. I think we just opened Pandora's Box."

"I do not understand," Rome said. "What is Pandora's Box?"

"You'd better hope we never find out," Rei replied, gravely.

A Preview of *Rebellion*
(The Rome's Revolution Saga: Book 2)

(12 months later)
Second Planet (Deucado), Tau Ceti System

REI AND ROME BOTH WATCHED WITH WIDE-EYED FASCINATION AS the blue jewel grew larger and larger. Whereas earlier, it had been marble-sized and then basketball-sized, now it was filling their whole field of view. They quickly passed into the night side.

Within their cabin, Rei and Rome heard the standard thump and delayed clunk as MINIMCOM reversed the orientation of his tug and fired his plasma thrusters, slowing the assembly gradually as they swung past the planet.

At last, MINIMCOM announced, "Orbit achieved."

Rei looked at Rome. "Honey, we're home," he said with a broad smile on his face.

Rome nodded and watched intently as they were coming up on the dawn side. Where the sun was illuminating the water, the deep blue oceans sparkled crisply from their high angle. Although there were large sections covered by heavy white clouds, much of the planet's surface was easily viewed. This planet had roughly an equal distribution of land and water. The majority of the land mass was contained within two major continents, with the one divided nearly in half with a relatively narrow isthmus connecting the northern and southern halves. As they moved around past the ocean and over the land, they could see the one continent had a Swiss cheese-like appearance. All across the surface there were many, many lakes and inland seas, most of them circular or rounded.

"Look at all the holes," Rei said.

"Yes. Despite what MINIMCOM said about a shield, they must be due to a substantial number of collisions with comets and such," Rome observed.

"Most of them seem soft, not sharp like you see on the moon. Have there been any reports of bombardment since the Vuduri have been here?" Rei asked.

"Not that I am aware of."

"Well, it looks good to me," Rei said. "There and there," he pointed down, "there's a ton of bright yellow and green coloration. That has to be vegetation."

"Oh yes, there is much vegetation," Rome replied.

Without warning, the central display lit up and in front of them sat a gray-haired Vuduri man.

"Who are you?" he asked in Vuduri. "We do not detect any PPT resonance."

"We are mandasurte," Rome answered. "We have come from the Tabit stellar observatory. We are towing one of the ancient Essessoni Arks that we found there."

The man's eyes grew wide then narrowed. In a flat voice, he said, "On this world, mandasurte in possession of Vuduri technology is a capital crime. You have condemned yourself. You will die."

The screen went black.

"What the hell!?" Rei shouted.

The MIDAR display lit up.

`"The Vuduri have just launched multiple craft. They appear to be armed."`

"Vuduri do not use weapons," Rome insisted.

`"These do."`

"Forget that. What do we do? MINIMCOM, can we outrun them?" Rei asked, his voice rising.

`"Not with your cargo craft."`

"And if we left it here?"

`"Rome already told them it was an Ark. They will assume the Erklirte have returned."`

"Can you get them back on the comm?" Rome asked, desperately. "Their rules should not apply to us. We are supposed to be here."

`"I have already tried. There is no reply. You should determine a course of action and quickly. I believe you should take evasive maneuvers immediately!"`

"What kind of arms are they carrying?" Rei asked anxiously.

`"Magnetic pulse cannons, electrostatic charge disrupters and PPT throwers."`

Rome gasped. All the color left her face.

"What? Say again." Rei said.

`"PPT throwers."`

"What are those?" Rei asked, panicked.

`"They are normally used in mining and salvage operations on the surface. They create a moving PPT tunnel. They can cut through any material known to man. However, in space, they can extend over a much greater distance."`

"So you're saying…" Rei sputtered.

"What he is saying," Rome barked, "is that they are for slicing up very large objects into very tiny pieces."

www.ingramcontent.com/pod-product-compliance
Lightning Source LLC
Chambersburg PA
CBHW022111170626
46808CB00002B/686